AMERICAN SCHOOL TEXTBOOK

GRADE 3

MP3

Reading & Writing

作者 Christine Dugan / Leslie Huber / Margot Kinberg / Miriam Meyers 譯者 黃詩韻

FUN 學美國英語 閱讀寫作 課本 3
American School Textbook: *Reading & Writing*

作　　者　Christine Dugan / Leslie Huber / Margot Kinberg / Miriam Meyers
審　　定　Judy Majewski
譯　　者　黃詩韻
編　　輯　呂紹柔

封面設計　郭瀞暄
內文排版　田慧盈／郭瀞暄
製程管理　宋建文
出 版 者　寂天文化事業股份有限公司
電　　話　+886-(0)2-2365-9739
傳　　真　+886-(0)2-2365-9835
網　　址　www.icosmos.com.tw
讀者服務　onlineservice@icosmos.com.tw
出版日期　2013 年 8 月 初版一刷　(080101)

郵撥帳號　1998620-0　寂天文化事業股份有限公司

- 劃撥金額 600（含）元以上者，郵資免費。
- 訂購金額 600 元以下者，加收 65 元運費。

【若有破損，請寄回更換，謝謝。】

HOW TO USE THIS BOOK

The **Skill Overview** provides background information about the skill focus for the lesson.

Reading Passage

The **Lesson Number** and **Reading Skill** are clearly identified.

The **Reading Tip** provides guidance for reading each lesson.

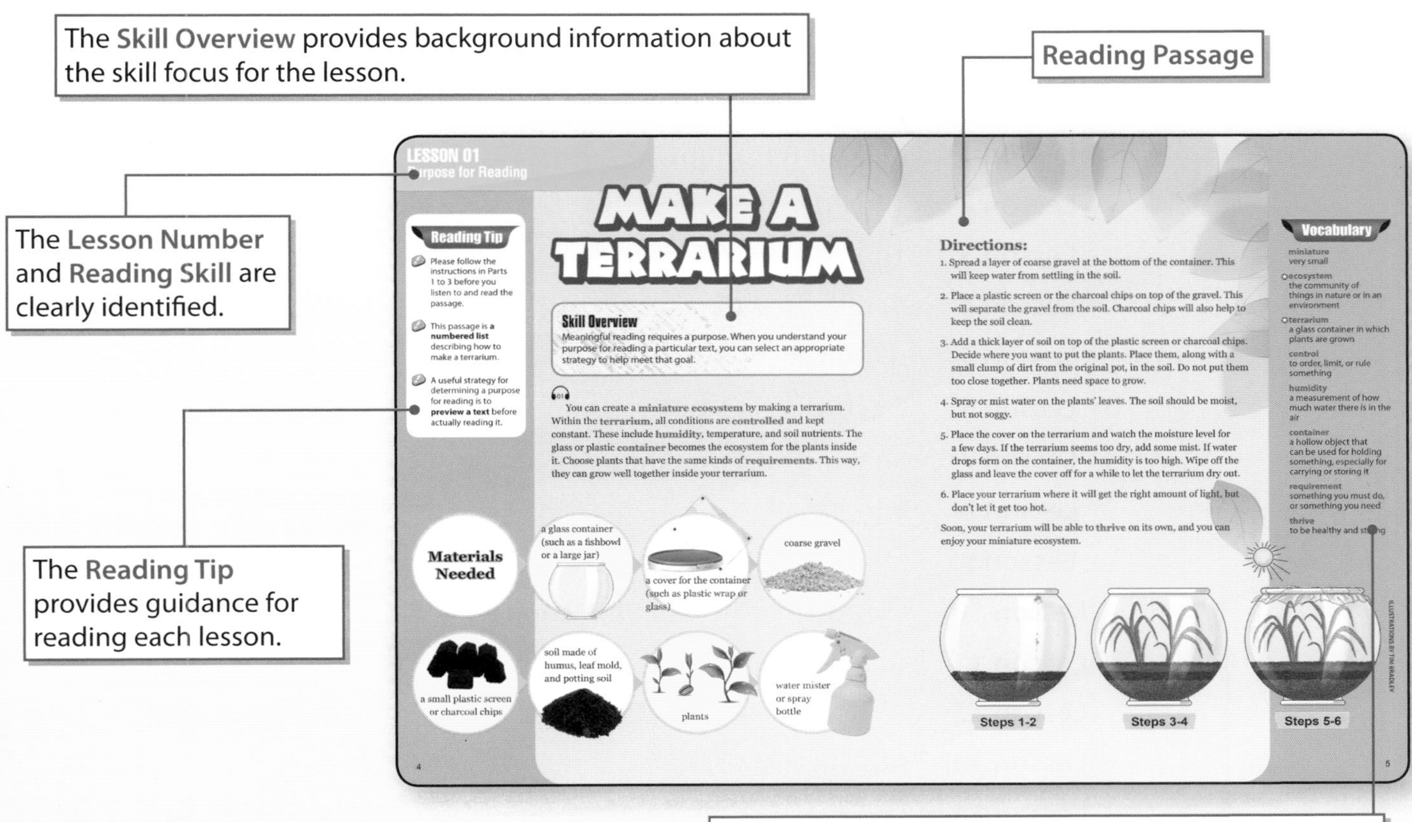

LESSON 01
Purpose for Reading

Reading Tip

- Please follow the instructions in Parts 1 to 3 before you listen to and read the passage.
- This passage is a **numbered list** describing how to make a terrarium.
- A useful strategy for determining a purpose for reading is to **preview a text** before actually reading it.

MAKE A TERRARIUM

Skill Overview
Meaningful reading requires a purpose. When you understand your purpose for reading a particular text, you can select an appropriate strategy to help meet that goal.

You can create a **miniature ecosystem** by making a terrarium. Within the **terrarium**, all conditions are **controlled** and kept constant. These include **humidity**, temperature, and soil nutrients. The glass or plastic **container** becomes the ecosystem for the plants inside it. Choose plants that have the same kinds of **requirements**. This way, they can grow well together inside your terrarium.

Materials Needed

- a glass container (such as a fishbowl or a large jar)
- a cover for the container (such as plastic wrap or glass)
- coarse gravel
- a small plastic screen or charcoal chips
- soil made of humus, leaf mold, and potting soil
- plants
- water mister or spray bottle

Directions:

1. Spread a layer of coarse gravel at the bottom of the container. This will keep water from settling in the soil.
2. Place a plastic screen or the charcoal chips on top of the gravel. This will separate the gravel from the soil. Charcoal chips will also help to keep the soil clean.
3. Add a thick layer of soil on top of the plastic screen or charcoal chips. Decide where you want to put the plants. Place them, along with a small clump of dirt from the original pot, in the soil. Do not put them too close together. Plants need space to grow.
4. Spray or mist water on the plants' leaves. The soil should be moist, but not soggy.
5. Place the cover on the terrarium and watch the moisture level for a few days. If the terrarium seems too dry, add some mist. If water drops form on the container, the humidity is too high. Wipe off the glass and leave the cover off for a while to let the terrarium dry out.
6. Place your terrarium where it will get the right amount of light, but don't let it get too hot.

Soon, your terrarium will be able to **thrive** on its own, and you can enjoy your miniature ecosystem.

Steps 1-2 | Steps 3-4 | Steps 5-6

Vocabulary

- miniature: very small
- ecosystem: the community of things in nature or in an environment
- terrarium: a glass container in which plants are grown
- control: to order, limit, or rule something
- humidity: a measurement of how much water there is in the air
- container: a hollow object that can be used for holding something, especially for carrying or storing it
- requirement: something you must do, or something you need
- thrive: to be healthy and strong

ILLUSTRATIONS BY TIM BRADLEY

4 | 5

Critical Vocabulary words from the passage are listed.

Power Up summarizes the key terminology and ideas for each lesson.

Comprehension Review helps determine your level of mastery of these strategies and skills.

Word Power reinforces the importance of the critical vocabularies with pictures.

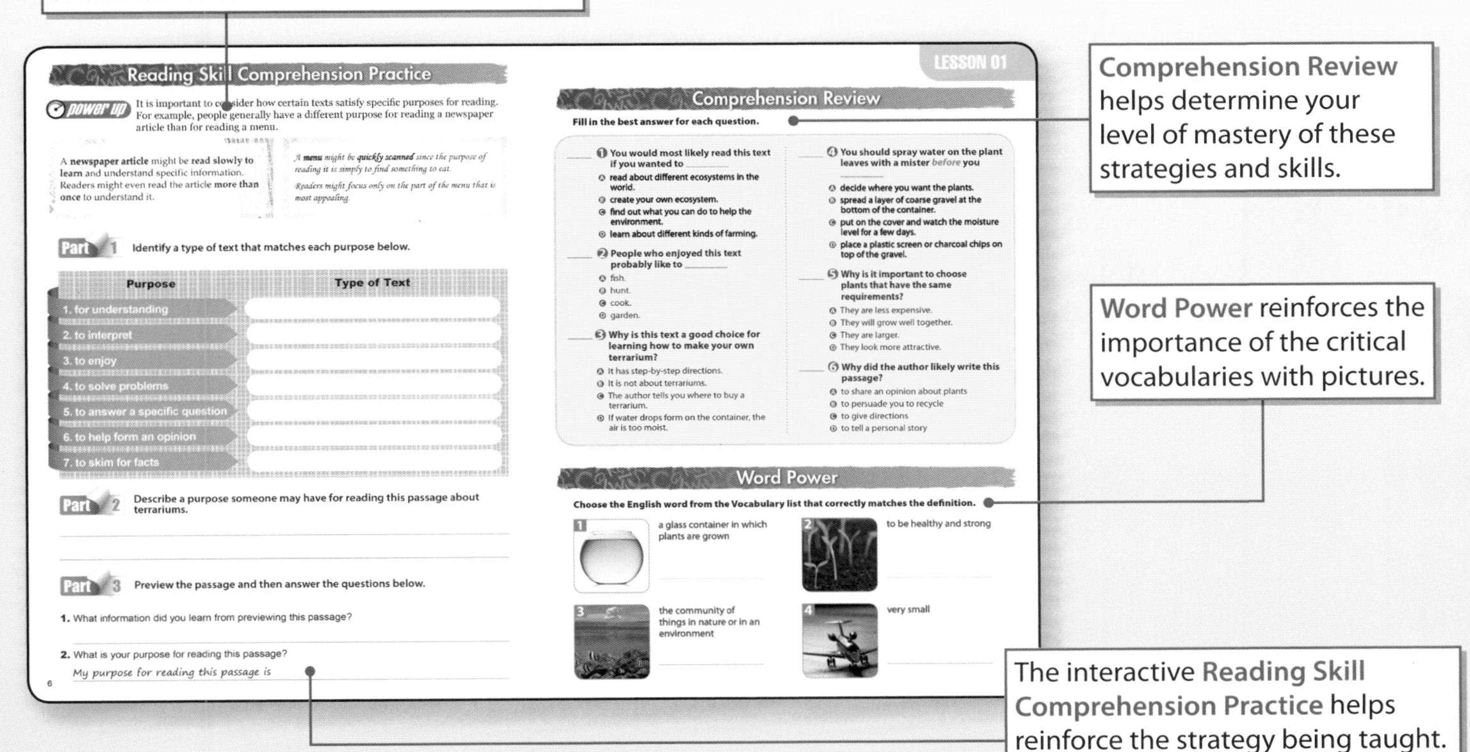

Reading Skill Comprehension Practice

power up: It is important to consider how certain texts satisfy specific purposes for reading. For example, people generally have a different purpose for reading a newspaper article than for reading a menu.

A **newspaper article** might be **read slowly** to **learn** and understand specific information. Readers might even read the article **more than once** to understand it.

A ***menu*** *might be* ***quickly scanned*** *since the purpose of reading it is simply to find something to eat. Readers might focus only on the part of the menu that is most appealing.*

Part 1 Identify a type of text that matches each purpose below.

Purpose	Type of Text
1. for understanding	
2. to interpret	
3. to enjoy	
4. to solve problems	
5. to answer a specific question	
6. to help form an opinion	
7. to skim for facts	

Part 2 Describe a purpose someone may have for reading this passage about terrariums.

Part 3 Preview the passage and then answer the questions below.

1. What information did you learn from previewing this passage?
2. What is your purpose for reading this passage?
My purpose for reading this passage is

6

LESSON 01

Comprehension Review

Fill in the best answer for each question.

1. You would most likely read this text if you wanted to ______
   - a. read about different ecosystems in the world.
   - b. create your own ecosystem.
   - c. find out what you can do to help the environment.
   - d. learn about different kinds of farming.
2. People who enjoyed this text probably like to ______
   - a. fish.
   - b. hunt.
   - c. cook.
   - d. garden.
3. Why is this text a good choice for learning how to make your own terrarium?
   - a. It has step-by-step directions.
   - b. It is not about terrariums.
   - c. The author tells you where to buy a terrarium.
   - d. If water drops form on the container, the air is too moist.
4. You should spray water on the plant leaves with a mister *before* you ______
   - a. decide where you want the plants.
   - b. spread a layer of coarse gravel at the bottom of the container.
   - c. put on the cover and watch the moisture level for a few days.
   - d. place a plastic screen or charcoal chips on top of the gravel.
5. Why is it important to choose plants that have the same requirements?
   - a. They are less expensive.
   - b. They will grow well together.
   - c. They are larger.
   - d. They look more attractive.
6. Why did the author likely write this passage?
   - a. to share an opinion about plants
   - b. to persuade you to recycle
   - c. to give directions
   - d. to tell a personal story

Word Power

Choose the English word from the Vocabulary list that correctly matches the definition.

1. a glass container in which plants are grown
2. to be healthy and strong
3. the community of things in nature or in an environment
4. very small

The interactive **Reading Skill Comprehension Practice** helps reinforce the strategy being taught.

Contents Chart

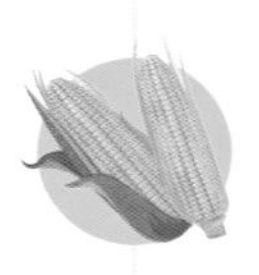

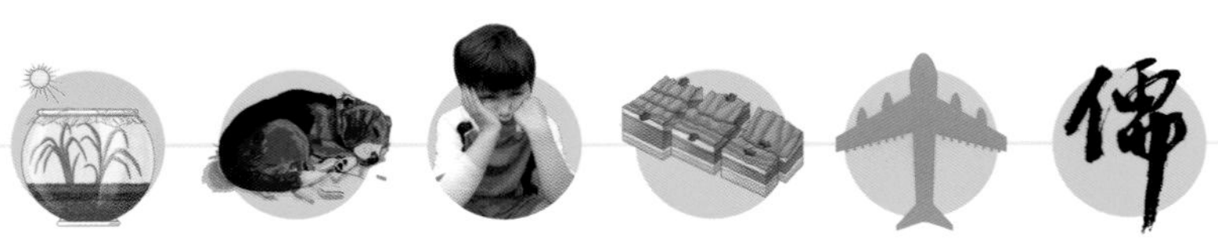

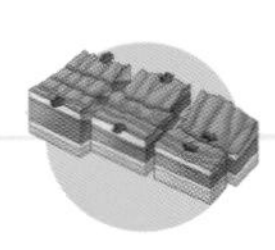

Reading Skill	Subject
Purpose for Reading	Science
Previewing	Social Studies ★ History and Geography
Conflict and Resolution	Language and Literature
Making Inferences	Social Studies ★ History and Geography
Main Idea and Details	Social Studies ★ History and Geography
Titles to Predict	Science
Selecting Reading Material	Science
Character Development	Language and Literature
Sequential Order	Social Studies ★ History and Geography
Headings to Determine Main Ideas	Social Studies ★ History and Geography
Topic Sentences to Predict	Science
Literary Devices	Language and Literature
Cause and Effect	Social Studies ★ History and Geography
Paraphrasing	Language and Literature
Summary Sentences	Language and Literature
Reflecting on What Has Been Learned	Science
Use of Language	Language and Literature
Compare and Contrast	Social Studies ★ History and Geography
Adjust and Extend Knowledge	Social Studies ★ History and Geography
Typeface	Social Studies ★ History and Geography
Author's Devices	Language and Literature
Author's Point of View	Language and Literature
Drawing Conclusions	Language and Literature
Proposition and Support	Social Studies ★ History and Geography
Captions to Determine Main Ideas	Social Studies ★ History and Geography
Monitoring Reading Strategies	Social Studies ★ History and Geography
Chapter Titles to Determine Main Ideas	Social Studies ★ History and Geography
Chronological Order	Social Studies ★ History and Geography
Fact and Opinion	Language and Literature
Questioning	Science

MAKE A TERRARIUM

Reading Tip

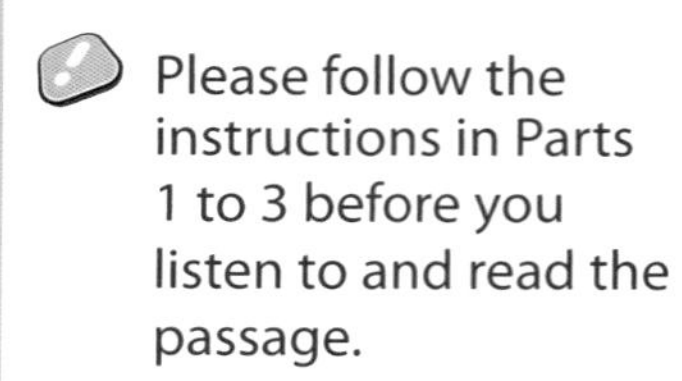

Please follow the instructions in Parts 1 to 3 before you listen to and read the passage.

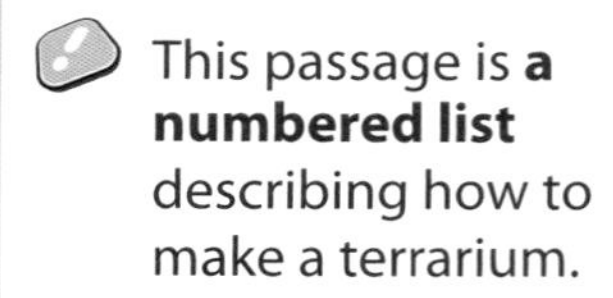

This passage is **a numbered list** describing how to make a terrarium.

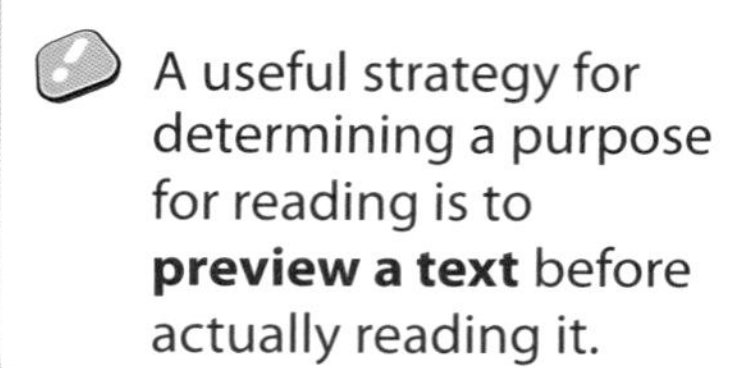

A useful strategy for determining a purpose for reading is to **preview a text** before actually reading it.

Skill Overview

Meaningful reading requires a purpose. When you understand your purpose for reading a particular text, you can select an appropriate strategy to help meet that goal.

You can create a **miniature ecosystem** by making a terrarium. Within the **terrarium**, all conditions are **controlled** and kept constant. These include **humidity**, temperature, and soil nutrients. The glass or plastic **container** becomes the ecosystem for the plants inside it. Choose plants that have the same **requirements**. This way, they can grow well together inside your terrarium.

Materials Needed

a glass container (such as a fishbowl or a large jar)

a cover for the container (such as plastic wrap or glass)

coarse gravel

a small plastic screen or charcoal chips

soil made of humus, leaf mold, and potting soil

plants

water mister or spray bottle

Directions:

1. Spread a layer of coarse gravel at the bottom of the container. This will keep water from settling in the soil.
2. Place a plastic screen or the charcoal chips on top of the gravel. This will separate the gravel from the soil. Charcoal chips will also help to keep the soil clean.
3. Add a thick layer of soil on top of the plastic screen or charcoal chips. Decide where you want to put the plants. Place them, along with a small clump of dirt from the original pot, in the soil. Do not put them too close together. Plants need space to grow.
4. Spray or mist water on the plants' leaves. The soil should be moist, but not soggy.
5. Place the cover on the terrarium and watch the moisture level for a few days. If the terrarium seems too dry, add some mist. If water drops form on the container, the humidity is too high. Wipe off the glass and leave the cover off for a while to let the terrarium dry out.
6. Place your terrarium where it will get the right amount of light, but don't let it get too hot.

Soon, your terrarium will be able to **thrive** on its own, and you can enjoy your miniature ecosystem.

Vocabulary

miniature
very small

✪**ecosystem**
the community of things in nature or in an environment

✪**terrarium**
a glass container in which plants are grown

control
to order, limit, or rule something

humidity
a measurement of how much water there is in the air

container
a hollow object that can be used for holding something, especially for carrying or storing it

requirement
something you must do, or something you need

thrive
to be healthy and strong

Steps 1-2

Steps 3-4

Steps 5-6

ILLUSTRATIONS BY TIM BRADLEY

Reading Skill Comprehension Practice

It is important to consider how certain texts satisfy specific purposes for reading. For example, people generally have a different purpose for reading a newspaper article than for reading a menu.

A **newspaper article** might be **read slowly to learn** and understand specific information. Readers might even read the article **more than once** to understand it.

*A **menu** might be **quickly scanned** since the purpose of reading it is simply to find something to eat.*

Readers might focus only on the part of the menu that is most appealing.

Identify a type of text that matches each purpose below.

Purpose	Type of Text
1. for understanding	
2. to interpret	
3. to enjoy	
4. to solve problems	
5. to answer a specific question	
6. to help form an opinion	
7. to skim for facts	

Describe a purpose someone may have for reading this passage about terrariums.

____

____

Preview the passage and then answer the questions below.

1. What information did you learn from previewing this passage?

____

2. What is your purpose for reading this passage?

My purpose for reading this passage is ______________________________

Comprehension Review

Fill in the best answer for each question.

_____ **1 You would most likely read this text if you wanted to _____**

- Ⓐ read about different ecosystems in the world.
- Ⓑ create your own ecosystem.
- Ⓒ find out what you can do to help the environment.
- Ⓓ learn about different kinds of farming.

_____ **2 People who enjoyed this text probably like to _____**

- Ⓐ fish.
- Ⓑ hunt.
- Ⓒ cook.
- Ⓓ garden.

_____ **3 Why is this text a good choice for learning how to make your own terrarium?**

- Ⓐ It has step-by-step directions.
- Ⓑ It is not about terrariums.
- Ⓒ The author tells you where to buy a terrarium.
- Ⓓ If water drops form on the container, the air is too moist.

_____ **4 You should spray water on the plant leaves with a mister *before* you _____**

- Ⓐ decide where you want the plants.
- Ⓑ spread a layer of coarse gravel at the bottom of the container.
- Ⓒ put on the cover and watch the moisture level for a few days.
- Ⓓ place a plastic screen or charcoal chips on top of the gravel.

_____ **5 Why is it important to choose plants that have the same requirements?**

- Ⓐ They are less expensive.
- Ⓑ They will grow well together.
- Ⓒ They are larger.
- Ⓓ They look more attractive.

_____ **6 Why did the author likely write this passage?**

- Ⓐ to share an opinion about plants
- Ⓑ to persuade you to recycle
- Ⓒ to give directions
- Ⓓ to tell a personal story

Word Power

Choose the English word from the Vocabulary list that correctly matches the definition.

a glass container in which plants are grown

____

to be healthy and strong

____

the community of things in nature or in an environment

____

very small

____

The Price to Play

Reading Tip

- Look quickly at the passage, and see what you can determine from its format. Please follow the instructions in Parts 1 and 2 before you listen to and read the passage.
- One effective way to preview material is by **skimming** it. Skimming may include **reading a few words, a sentence, the title, or the headings** to get a sense of what is included in the passage.

Skill Overview

Previewing text includes **looking at features** such as the title, headings, photos, graphic, and layout. Readers who preview text can also **activate their prior knowledge** and apply what they already know to what they want to learn from the text.

02

Kevin Donnelly plays soccer. Boy, does he play soccer! Not long ago, the New Jersey boy spent all weekend on the soccer field—three games on Saturday and three on Sunday.

Sound familiar? Forty million kids play **organized** sports. But it's not just the number of kids playing that's amazing. Parents are spending more and more money and time on their kids' sports careers. Kevin's parents will pay about $3,000 this year for him to play soccer. That includes club **dues**, private clinics, summer camps, and travel.

Many parents pay top dollar so their kids can have the best private lessons and **equipment**. Others spend hours driving their kids to games. Has the love of competition gone too far? Or are the **benefits** of team sports worth the huge costs and intense pressure to win?

Some experts say that kids benefit from playing team sports as long as they are having fun. "We know from a lot of research that kids who participate in sports tend to do better academically," says Mark Goldstein. He is a child psychologist at Roosevelt University in Chicago, Illinois. "It forces them to be more organized with their time and to prioritize a lot better."

But pushy parents and harsh coaches can take all the fun out of playing. Many say that is why 73 percent of kids quit sports by age 13. "They stop playing because it **ceases** to be fun, and the pressure put on them by coaches and parents doesn't make it worthwhile," says Fred Engh. Engh is a coach and author of the book *Why Johnny Hates Sports*.

Even worse, **injuries** from intense competition seem to be on the rise. The Consumer Product Safety Commission **reports** that four million kids end up in hospital emergency rooms for sports-related injuries each year. Eight million more are treated for medical problems caused by sports.

Some parents hope their kids' athletic skills will win them college scholarship money. This does not seem realistic. Fewer than 1 percent of kids playing sports today will earn a college scholarship.

The critics sound like a bunch of sore losers to families who live for sports. They say the joy of sports can't be **measured** in dollars and cents—or runs and goals. "It's my life," says Aidan Wolfe, 10, who plays soccer in Portland, Oregon. "I love soccer. If my parents told me I couldn't play anymore, I'd be devastated."

organized
neatly arranged or carefully planned

dues
the official payments that you make to an organization you belong to

equipment
a set of necessary tools, clothing, etc., for a particular purpose

benefit
a positive effect of doing something

cease
to stop

injury
physical harm or damage to someone's body caused by an accident or an attack

report
to give a description of something or information about it

measure
to discover the exact size or amount of something

Reading Skill Comprehension Practice

Preview the passage and then answer the questions below.

1. What does the **title** tell you about the topic of the passage?

The Price to Play

The title tells me ____________________

2. Is the passage written in **paragraphs**?

____

3. What do the pictures tell you about the topic of the passage?

The pictures tell me ____________________

____

____

Part 2 **Record what you noticed as you skimmed the passage about playing sports.**

____

____

Explain how previewing the passage helped your comprehension as you read.

____

____

____

____

Comprehension Review

Fill in the best answer for each question.

_____ **1 The title and picture tell you that this passage is about _____**

Ⓐ saving money.
Ⓑ playing basketball.
Ⓒ getting a part-time job.
Ⓓ playing sports.

_____ **2 This passage has no numbered lists, so it is probably *not* _____**

Ⓐ a newspaper article.
Ⓑ a recipe or set of instructions.
Ⓒ a story about sports.
Ⓓ a magazine article.

_____ **3 This passage will probably be interesting to someone who _____**

Ⓐ likes politics.
Ⓑ hates basketball.
Ⓒ plays sports.
Ⓓ is interested in science.

_____ **4 What is the problem in this passage?**

Ⓐ Sports may put too much pressure on kids.
Ⓑ There are not enough sports teams.
Ⓒ Too many coaches do not let kids play.
Ⓓ Kids who like sports do not get enough help from their parents.

_____ **5 Which of these is an opinion?**

Ⓐ Forty million kids play organized sports.
Ⓑ The Consumer Product Safety Commission reports that four million kids end up in hospital emergency rooms for sports-related injuries each year.
Ⓒ He is a child psychologist at Roosevelt University.
Ⓓ The critics sound like a bunch of sore losers.

_____ **6 For some kids, _____ take the fun out of playing sports.**

Ⓐ soccer games
Ⓑ pushy parents and harsh coaches
Ⓒ child psychologists
Ⓓ forty million kids

Word Power

Choose the English word from the Vocabulary list that correctly matches the definition.

1 a positive effect of doing something

____

2 to stop

____

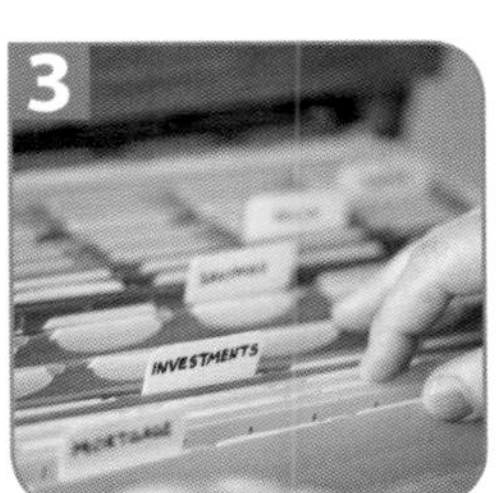

3 neatly arranged or carefully planned

____

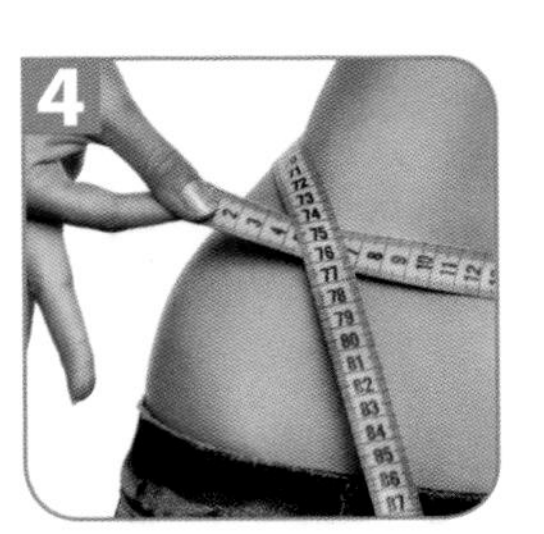

4 to discover the exact size or amount of something

____

Reading Tip

- This passage has a conflict and a resolution. Authors use conflict and resolution to **develop the plot of a story**.
- Please listen to and read paragraphs 1 to 4, and then follow the instructions in Part 1 before you finish the rest of the passage.

Skill Overview

Narrative text often features a conflict or problem and describes how the problem is resolved. Successful readers identify conflict and resolution in a story and use appropriate strategies to better understand the text.

The Hardest Words to Say

03

In my family, the words "I love you" are never said. It's not that we don't love each other; we just show it without saying it. I help my sister learn her multiplication tables, and I collect my baby brother's vegetables from under his chair. My mom puts oatmeal raisin cookies in my lunch, and my dad takes me to tractor-pull **exhibitions**.

Then the puppy came, and I don't think I'd ever heard "I love you" so much. "Where's my lovey-dovey Shadow?" Mom would croon. And she practically held his aluminum dog bowl while Shadow scattered food all over the kitchen floor.

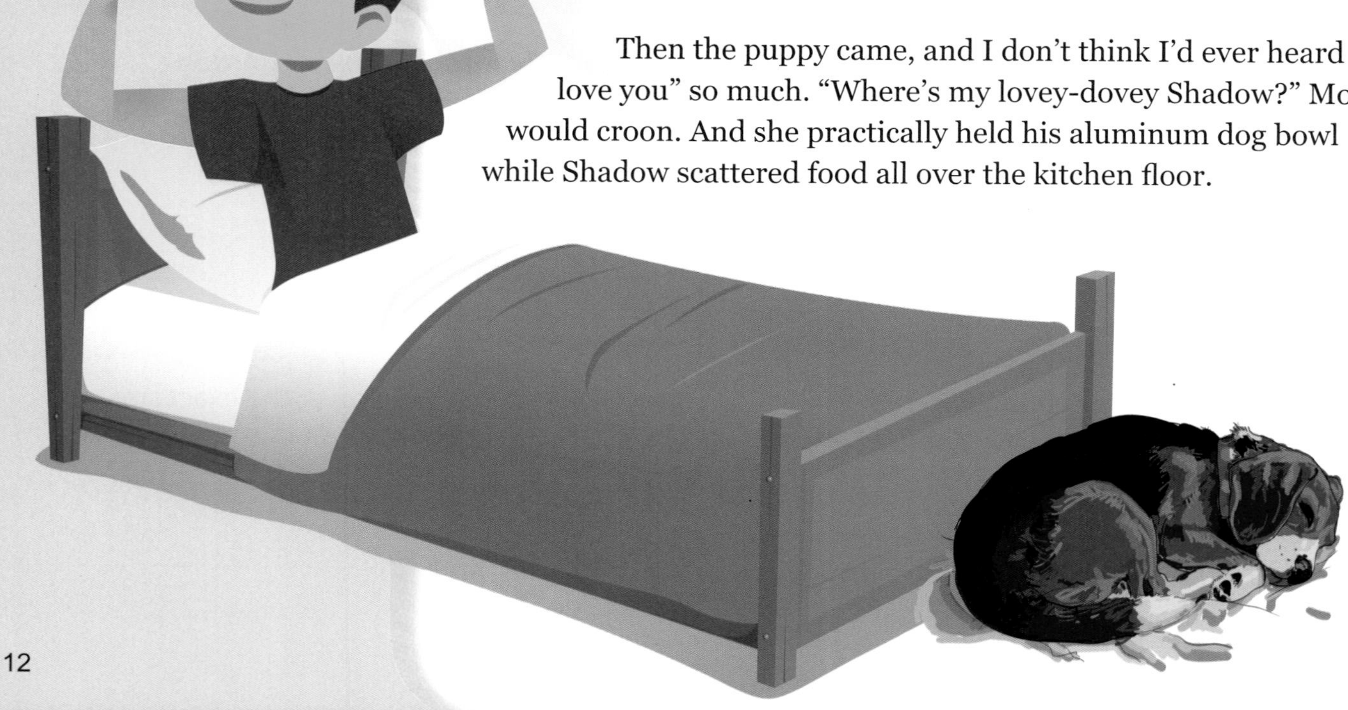

Arriving home, my dad would shout, "Where's my boy, where's my boy?" and Shadow would speed around the corner and run between his legs a million times.

At night, with Shadow **curled** into a ball at the foot of my bed, I even **whispered**, "Good night, Shadow. I love you." It felt wonderful to show and tell love, and somehow I slept better after doing that.

Last night, after my mom and dad squished the covers under my neck, I **murmured**, "I love you." When their **silhouettes** froze in the doorway, I suddenly hoped they hadn't heard me. I **imagined** my heart beating through the covers, and I twisted away so my blanket **shielded** my eyes.

The next day, Dad came home early and shouted, "Where's my boy?" I bit the inside of my lip and continued playing Go Fish with my sister as Shadow scampered in and out of Dad's legs.

Dad sat down on the floor, hugged me tightly, and said, "No, here's my boy." Then he said, "I love you, Jonah."

My mother sat down with us and sorted the cards, but looked first at me and my sister. "You know I love you both, more than you can ever imagine," she said, tears trickling down her cheeks.

"Oh, Mommy, you are silly!" my sister giggled.

"Hey," my dad said, "how about you and me pitching some balls at the park?"

I grabbed my baseball glove from the closet and tossed my father the ball. "Where's Shadow's leash? He loves chasing balls."

"No, this is our time, Jonah—you and me," my dad said as we walked to the door, Shadow tripping along excitedly behind us.

"Ah, Dad, can't we bring Shadow?" I begged. Dad nodded, I grabbed Shadow's leash, and the three of us headed to the park. After all, how could I go without the one who showed us how to truly **express** love?

Vocabulary

exhibition
public showing of something

curl
to make something into the shape of a circle

whisper
to speak very quietly, using the breath but not the voice

murmur
to mumble or say something in a quiet voice

silhouette
the shaded outline of something

imagine
to form or have a mental picture or idea of something

shield
to protect someone or something

express
to show a feeling, opinion, or fact

Reading Skill Comprehension Practice

Part 1 Explain the conflict in this passage. Then predict how the author will resolve this conflict.

The conflict in this story is that . . .; I predict that . . .

____

____

____

Part 2 Explain the resolution of this conflict. Then tell how the resolution was similar to or different from your prediction in Part 1.

____

____

____

____

Part 3 Read the passage from Lesson 8. Write the title and then fill in the graphic organizer below.

Title: ______________________________

CONFLICT	RESOLUTION

Comprehension Review

Fill in the best answer for each question.

_____ **1 The conflict in this story is about _____**

- A expressing love.
- B taking care of Shadow.
- C playing baseball.
- D doing chores.

_____ **2 The conflict starts when _____**

- A Jonah's parents forget his birthday.
- B Shadow gets to go to the park with Jonah and his father.
- C Jonah realizes that everyone in the family shows love to Shadow.
- D Jonah's mother gets lost.

_____ **3 The conflict is resolved when _____**

- A Shadow runs away.
- B Jonah's parents tell Jonah and his sister they love them.
- C Jonah and his sister play Go Fish.
- D Jonah and Shadow play ball in the park.

_____ **4 Jonah probably felt _____ when his father said, "No, here's my boy."**

- A sad
- B angry
- C jealous
- D surprised

_____ **5 *When their silhouettes froze in the doorway, I suddenly hoped they hadn't heard me.***

What does the word <u>*silhouettes*</u> mean in this sentence?

- A dogs
- B words
- C shadows or outlines
- D children

_____ **6 This story is told from _____ point of view.**

- A Jonah's sister's
- B Jonah's
- C Shadow's
- D Jonah's father's

Word Power

Choose the English word from the Vocabulary list that correctly matches the definition.

to mumble or say something in a quiet voice

____

the shaded outline of something

____

to show a feeling, opinion, or fact

____

public showing of something

____

Benjamin Banneker

Benjamin Banneker

Reading Tip

- An **inference** is a **conclusion** that is made based on facts in a text.
- In this passage, you are going to read a biography of an African American scientist, inventor, and mathematician named Benjamin Banneker.

Skill Overview

Making inferences is the process of **judging**, **concluding**, or **reasoning** based on given information. Successful readers are able to look beyond the author's words and understand the real message of a text.

04

"Divide 60 into four such parts that the first being increased by 4, the second decreased by 4, the third multiplied by 4, the fourth part divided by 4, that the sum, the difference, the product and the quotient shall be one and the same number."

This mathematical puzzle was created by a special person. He was an African American scientist, inventor, and mathematician. His name was Benjamin Banneker. His life was as **remarkable** as his **accomplishments**.

Banneker was born in Maryland in 1731. His father was a freed slave. His mother was an Englishwoman who owned a farm. Banneker worked hard on the farm as a boy. After his grandmother taught him to read, he wanted to learn more. He was interested in many things. He liked music, math, and inventing. Around the age of 20, Banneker built a clock **from scratch**. The clock kept perfect time for the rest of his life!

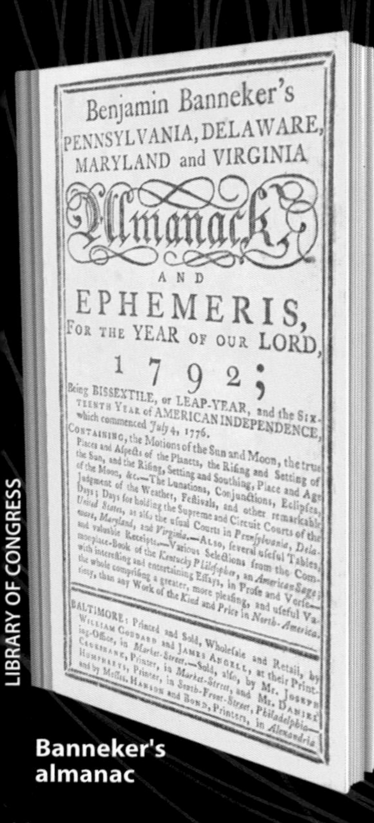

Benjamin Banneker's
PENNSYLVANIA, DELAWARE,
MARYLAND and VIRGINIA
Almanack
AND
EPHEMERIS,
FOR THE YEAR OF OUR LORD,
1792;
Being BISSEXTILE, or LEAP-YEAR, and the SIXTEENTH YEAR of AMERICAN INDEPENDENCE, which commenced July 4, 1776.
CONTAINING, the Motions of the Sun and Moon, the true Places and Aspects of the Planets, the Rising and Setting of the Sun, and the Rising, Setting and Southing, Place and Age of the Moon, &c.—The Lunations, Conjunctions, Eclipses, Judgment of the Weather, Festivals, and other remarkable Days; Days for holding the Supreme and Circuit Courts of the United States, as also the usual Courts in Pennsylvania, Delaware, Maryland, and Virginia.—ALSO, several useful Tables, and valuable Receipts.—Various Selections from the Commonplace-Book of the Kentucky Philosopher, an American Sage; with interesting and entertaining Essays, in Prose and Verse—the whole comprising a greater, more pleasing, and useful Variety, than any Work of the Kind and Price in North-America.
BALTIMORE: Printed and Sold, Wholesale and Retail, by WILLIAM GODDARD and JAMES ANGELL, at their Printing-Office, in Market-Street.—Sold, also, by Mr. JOSEPH CRUIKSHANK, Printer, in Market-Street, and Mr. DANIEL HUMPHREYS, Printer, in South-Front-Street, Philadelphia—and by Messrs. HANSON and BOND, Printers, in Alexandria.

Banneker's almanac

At the age of 57, Banneker taught himself **algebra**, geometry, and trigonometry. He learned how to use astronomical instruments. These helped him figure out the movements of stars and planets. Just for fun, he used math to predict solar eclipses (when the Moon blocks out the Sun). Banneker used what he learned to **publish** an **almanac**. It **predicted** the hours of sunrise and sunset. It also had tables for predicting the high and low tides in Chesapeake Bay. It was sold to many people, including farmers.

Designing a City

In 1791, the new capital of the United States, Washington, D.C., was being designed. At that time, Banneker was known as a great mathematician. He was asked to help survey the land. Later, the chief designer left the project. He took all the drawings of the plans with him. Banneker was able to draw them from memory. This is why the nation's capital looks the way it does.

Banneker was more than a mathematician and scientist. He worked to end slavery, too. He wrote to Thomas Jefferson, arguing that slavery was wrong. The two wrote back and forth for years. Banneker never stopped learning. He wrote a mathematical study of locusts. He also did experiments in his house. Sadly, the day Banneker died, his house burned down. Most of his papers were destroyed. What did survive is our memory of this **exceptional** person.

Vocabulary

remarkable
extraordinary or surprising

accomplishment
skill or effort that led to success

from scratch
from the beginning or starting from nothing

algebra
a part of mathematics in which signs and letters represent numbers

publish
to make information available to people, especially in a book, magazine, or newspaper

✪**almanac**
a book that contains information about the weather or astronomy for a given year

predict
to say that an event or action will happen in the future

exceptional
much greater than usual, especially in skill, intelligence, quality, etc.

Reading Skill Comprehension Practice

One way readers can make inferences and understand what they are reading is by **making personal connections** to the text.

When readers can relate a text to something they know or have experienced in their life, they can more easily infer information from that text.

Record any personal connections you may have to the passage about Benjamin Banneker.

1. ______________________
2. ______________________
3. ______________________
4. ______________________

Answer the questions below.

1. What **inferences** did you make while reading this passage?

____

2. What **evidence** in the passage helped you make these inferences?

____

____

Think about other texts that can be connected to this biography. List those books or articles below.

1. *I think another text that can be connected to this biography is a story about George Washington Carver.*
2. ______________________

Comprehension Review

Fill in the best answer for each question.

_____ **1 You can guess from reading this passage that Benjamin Banneker _____**

- A was born in Pennsylvania.
- B did not like to learn.
- C was curious.
- D owned slaves.

_____ **2 Benjamin Banneker probably _____**

- A had a very good memory.
- B draw badly.
- C did not enjoy science.
- D was not good at reading or writing.

_____ **3 *Benjamin Banneker published a popular almanac with tables predicting high and low tides.***
You can infer that _____

- A he was not good with numbers.
- B he liked tide pools.
- C this information was important to people during this time.
- D no one else was interested in this information.

_____ **4 *Around the age of 20, Banneker built a clock from scratch.***
What does *from scratch* mean?

- A rom scratching his head
- B from parts (he made it himself)
- C from itching
- D from a clockmaker

_____ **5 What happened to Benjamin Banneker's papers?**

- A They were destroyed when his house burned down.
- B They are in a library in Washington, D.C.
- C They are buried with Banneker.
- D They are in a museum in Maryland.

_____ **6 What is the purpose of this text?**

- A to get you to visit Maryland
- B to tell about Benjamin Banneker
- C to tell how Washington, D.C., was built
- D to tell about the American Revolution

Word Power

Choose the English word from the Vocabulary list that correctly matches the definition.

1

a book that contains information about the weather or astronomy for a given year

____

2

skill or effort that led to success

____

3

to make information available to people, especially in a book, magazine, or newspaper

____

4

extraordinary or surprising

____

Reading Tip

- The **main idea** is the most important message that an author wants to share with you.
- Authors often write so that the information is interesting and engaging to the reader, but not every detail is necessary for understanding the main idea.

Skill Overview

Distinguishing between relevant and irrelevant information in a text helps readers identify the main idea. Focusing on the relevant and important details also helps people to better comprehend what they are reading.

A Brief History of Planes

🎧05

Have you ever watched a bird and wished you could fly? It seems that people have always dreamed of flying. In fact, as early as the 1800s, people tried to make flying **machines**. What would be a good model for a plane? You might think that a bird's body would be the best model. Although many people tried this, machines made in this way did not work.

It was two brothers who finally made the flying dream come true. Orville and Wilbur Wright were the first to build a **powered** plane that could really fly. First, they had some problems to **solve**. Two of the problems were making an engine light enough to get off the ground and keeping the plane in the air once it got there. In December 1903, Orville flew the first powered plane, although it didn't fly very far. He didn't fly very high, but he did **succeed** in flying! In later years, the airplane was **improved** so that it could carry more people and fly farther.

When planes were first used, they were flown only over land. The **distance** an airplane could travel had **increased**, but planes still were not able to fly far, far away. Then in 1927, Charles Lindbergh flew a plane across the ocean, from New York to Paris, France. The trip took more than 33 hours to complete. He made the whole trip without sleeping. To stay awake, Lindbergh put his head out the window to get a blast of cold air on his face. When he made it to Paris, there was a big **celebration**. After the flight, he became a hero, and airplane travel was forever changed.

Vocabulary

machine
a human-made device that is composed of fixed and moving parts and performs tasks

★**powered**
operated by an engine or electricity rather than by hand

solve
to find an answer to a problem

succeed
to achieve something that you have been aiming for

improve
to (cause something to) get better

distance
the amount of space between two places

increase
to (make something) become larger in amount or size

celebration
a party marking a happy event that just happened or is about to happen

LIBRARY OF CONGRESS

Charles Lindbergh

Orville Wright

Wilbur Wright

The Wright brothers' plane at Kitty Hawk, North Carolina

Reading Skill Comprehension Practice

Part 1 Write three **relevant** details from the passage.

1. *Orville and Wilbur Wright were the first to build a powered plane that could really fly.*
2. ______
3. ______
4. ______

Part 2 Write three details from the passage that are **irrelevant**.

1. *Orville and Wilbur Wright were brothers.*
2. ______
3. ______
4. ______

Part 3 Select one detail you wrote down in Part 1 and state why it is relevant. Choose a detail from Part 2 and state why it is irrelevant.

Relevant Detail

______

______

Why?

______

______

Irrelevant Detail

______

______

Why?

______

______

Comprehension Review

Fill in the best answer for each question.

_____ **1 In 1927, who flew a plane across the ocean from New York to Paris?**
- A Orville Wright
- B Wilbur Wright
- C Charles Lindbergh
- D Wilbur and Orville Wright

_____ **2 What was one problem the Wright brothers had to solve?**
- A flying a plane across the ocean
- B meeting Charles Lindbergh
- C using a bird's body as a model for a plane
- D making an engine light enough to get off the ground

_____ **3 Who flew the first powered plane in 1903?**
- A Orville Wright
- B Wilbur Wright
- C Charles Lindbergh
- D Wilbur and Orville Wright

_____ **4 Which of these happened first?**
- A Orville Wright flew the first powered plane.
- B Charles Lindbergh flew across the ocean.
- C People tried unsuccessfully to make flying machines.
- D Charles Lindberg became a hero.

_____ **5 Based on the passage, readers can conclude that Charles Lindbergh was _____**
- A athletic.
- B adventurous.
- C greedy.
- D lazy.

_____ **6 How did Charles Lindbergh become a hero?**
- A He flew across the ocean.
- B He invented a powered plane.
- C He flew the first powered plane.
- D He used a bird's body as a model for a flying machine.

Word Power

Choose the English word from the Vocabulary list that correctly matches the definition.

1

operated by an engine or electricity rather than by hand

_____

2

a party marking a happy event that just happened or is about to happen

_____

3

to (cause something to) get better

_____

4

a human-made device that is composed of fixed and moving parts and performs tasks

_____

Reading Tip

Follow the instruction in Part 1 before you listen to and read the passage.

Electricity and Magnetism

Skill Overview

The title of a text can give the reader clues about the main idea. The title can also be used to make predictions about a text; doing this helps readers stay focused as they read to confirm or revise their predictions.

Electricity

An *electrical* **current** is the flow of **electrons** from one place to another. There must be an electrical **circuit** for a current to flow. A circuit is a closed loop of conducting material. Electricity can flow along it. There are two types of electricity. They are static and current.

Shuffle your feet across a carpet. Then touch your friend's hand. You may both feel a small shock. This shock is a tiny jolt of static electricity.

Electricity is at rest until it is able to move. It is called *static* when it is at rest.

A plasma ball

You move electrons from one surface to the other when you shuffle your feet on the carpet. This makes one surface have a positive **charge** and the other have a negative charge. This difference in charges is called a *potential difference*. When you touch your friend's hand, the jolt you feel is the electrons moving from one hand to the other. This evens out the potential difference. It makes both surfaces **neutral** again.

Current electricity is like a river that runs in a circle. The electrons are always moving. To see how that works, we need to understand **magnets**.

Magnetism

Have you ever played with magnets? Magnets create an **invisible force**. The force only affects some things. Iron is one of these things. Magnetic forces can move a piece of iron without anything touching the metal.

Magnetism can only reach so far, though. The reach of a magnet is called its *magnetic field*. Magnetic forces can only be felt within the field. The lines of force cannot be seen.

The first magnets were found in nature. Scientists began to wonder if they could make artificial ones. *Artificial* means something that is made by people.

One scientist found a way. In 1820, Hans Oersted placed a compass near an electrical current. He saw that the needle on the compass moved. The current had made a magnetic field. Oersted studied this some more. He found that electrical currents have magnetic fields.

Vocabulary

current
the movement of water, air, or electricity in a particular direction

electron
a small part of an atom that moves around the nucleus

circuit
something shaped somewhat like a circle, especially a route, path, or sports track

charge
the amount of electricity that an electrical device stores

neutral
having no electrical charge

magnet
an object made of iron or steel that is able to attract certain metals and produces an invisible magnetic field

invisible
impossible to see

force
physical, especially violent, strength or power

A magnetic field

Reading Skill Comprehension Practice

Part 1 Read the title of the passage. Write what you think you will read about in the passage.

Electricity and Magnetism   Electricity   Magnetism

____

____

Compare your predictions from Part 1 with the content of the passage.

1. *My predictions for the text were* ______________________________

2. *The text is actually about* ______________________________

3. *My predictions are similar to and/or different from the actual passage in the following ways:*

____

Part 3 Write some alternative titles for this passage.

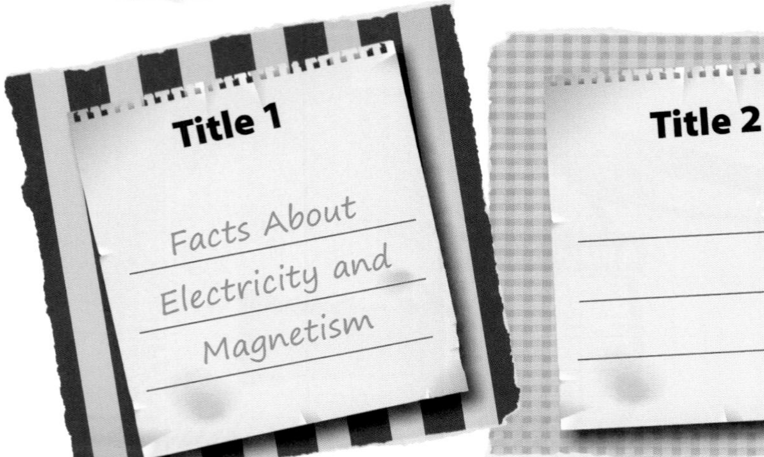

Comprehension Review

Fill in the best answer for each question.

_____ **1 The title tells you that you will read about _____**

- Ⓐ water power.
- Ⓑ electricity and magnets.
- Ⓒ iron.
- Ⓓ telephones and washing machines.

_____ **2 Electromagnetism has to do with _____**

- Ⓐ magnets.
- Ⓑ iron.
- Ⓒ electricity and magnetism.
- Ⓓ silver.

_____ **3 This passage is probably part of a _____**

- Ⓐ math book.
- Ⓑ social studies book.
- Ⓒ cookbook.
- Ⓓ science book.

_____ **4 The author likely wrote this passage to _____**

- Ⓐ show what a plasma ball looks like.
- Ⓑ teach readers about electricity and magnetism.
- Ⓒ get readers to do an experiment.
- Ⓓ tell about static electricity.

_____ **5 Why do you feel a jolt when you shuffle your feet on the carpet and then touch someone's hand?**

- Ⓐ Electrons are moving from one hand to the other.
- Ⓑ Your hand is magnetic.
- Ⓒ The carpet is magnetic.
- Ⓓ There are two types of electricity.

_____ **6 What did Oersted discover?**

- Ⓐ There are two types of electricity.
- Ⓑ Magnets create an invisible force.
- Ⓒ Electrical currents have magnetic fields.
- Ⓓ Current electricity is like a river that runs in a circle.

Word Power

Choose the English word from the Vocabulary list that correctly matches the definition.

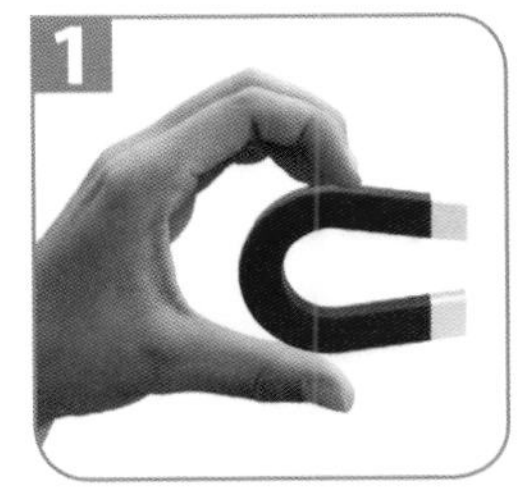

an object made of iron or steel that is able to attract certain metals and produces an invisible magnetic field

____

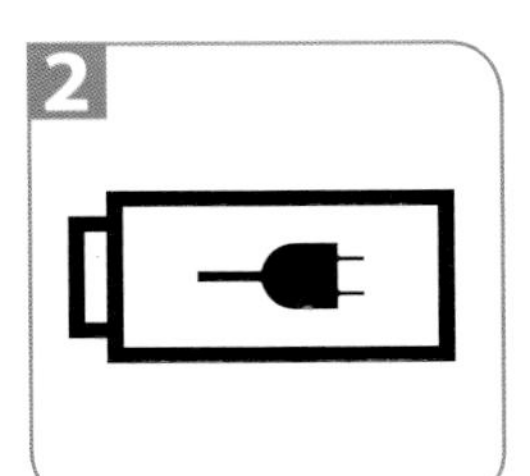

having no electrical charge

____

something shaped somewhat like a circle, especially a route, path, or sports track

____

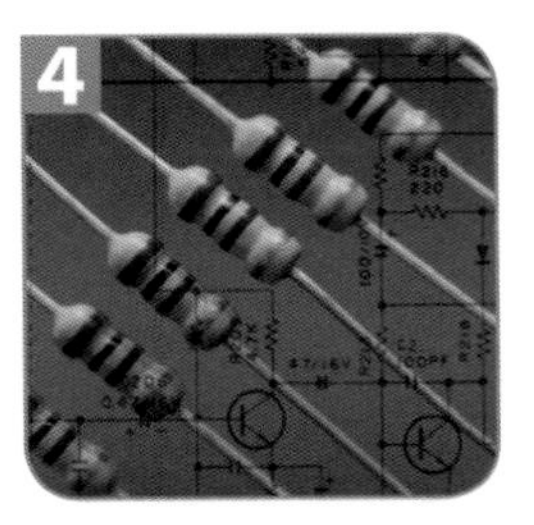

a small part of an atom that moves around the nucleus

____

Reading Tip

- Follow the instruction in Part 1 before you listen to and read the passage.
- The selection of reading material often requires careful consideration. **Personal interests** influence which materials you choose to read.

Skill Overview

A reader's selection of reading material helps him or her set a purpose for reading. When readers have a purpose for reading a particular text, they are able to focus on the content and have a better understanding of the text.

Shaking and Quaking

07

Earthquakes

If you live in certain parts of the world, you are very **familiar** with earthquakes. There's nothing quite like getting caught up in all the shaking and rolling that goes on when Earth makes a big shift. Have you ever felt an earthquake? An earthquake causes Earth's **surface** to move and **shift**. A large earthquake can change the land in seconds.

The outer shell of Earth's crust is broken up into many different pieces. As those pieces of the crust move, **stress** builds between them. The borders between pieces of crust are called *fault lines*. When too much stress builds along a **fault line**, the rock breaks or suddenly shifts. This is an earthquake.

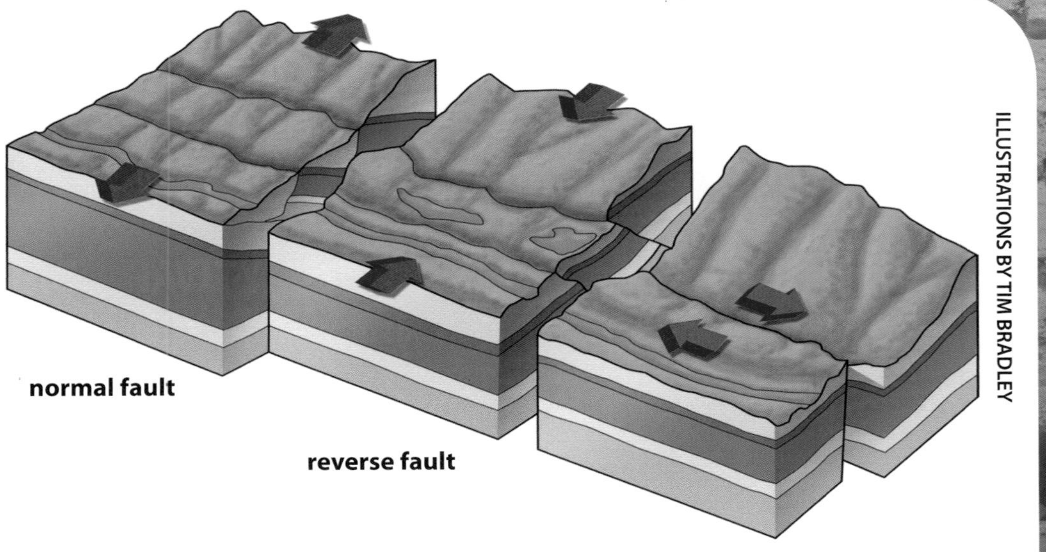

ILLUSTRATIONS BY TIM BRADLEY

Types of Faults

There are three main types of faults. A *normal fault* happens when the fault line in Earth's crust runs **at an angle** to the surface. The stress from an earthquake pushes out, away from the fault line. This causes one section of rock to drop below another section. The Rio Grande Valley in New Mexico is an example of a normal fault.

The Rio Grande Valley

A reverse fault also happens when the fault line is at an angle. But in this case, the stress from an earthquake pushes in toward the fault line. This causes one section of rock to move up and over another section. An example of a **reverse fault** can be found at Glacier National Park. A reverse fault is also called a *thrust fault*.

A *strike-slip fault* happens when the sections of rock on each side of the fault slip past each other sideways. There is little or no up-and-down **movement**. The San Andreas Fault in California is an example of a strike-slip fault.

The San Andreas Fault in California

Vocabulary

familiar
easy to recognize because of being seen, met, heard, etc., before

surface
the outer or top part or layer of something

shift
to move or change from one position or direction to another

stress
pressure on an object

✪**fault line**
the border between pieces of Earth's crust

at an angle
leaning or veering to the side rather than straight up or directly forward

✪**reverse fault**
two pieces of Earth's crust that are pushing toward each other, causing one piece to move up and over the other

movement
a change of position

Reading Skill Comprehension Practice

Part 1 Think about the topics covered in the passage. Explain your personal interest in them.

____

____

____

power up

Readers choose to read a text for a specific reason. Here are some of the possible reasons:

- **personal interest**
- **knowledge of the author**
- **text difficulty**
- **recommendations of others**

Part 2 Answer the questions below about what kinds of books you choose to read.

1. What is your favorite book? Why?

____

2. Who is your favorite author? Why?

____

3. Have you ever read a book recommended by another reader? If so, what was it and did you enjoy it?

____

4. How have your interests in reading materials changed over time?

____

Part 3 Write your book recommendation below.

I recommend the book "**A Song of Ice and Fire**" *because . . .*

I recommend the book ______________________________

____

____

____

Comprehension Review

Fill in the best answer for each question.

_____ **1 A person who likes __________ would probably find this passage interesting.**

- Ⓐ math
- Ⓑ animals
- Ⓒ history
- Ⓓ science

_____ **2 This passage would *not* be a good choice if you wanted to __________**

- Ⓐ read about fault lines.
- Ⓑ learn how to draw a map.
- Ⓒ read about earthquakes.
- Ⓓ learn how earthquakes happen.

_____ **3 If you were doing a report on __________, this passage would help you.**

- Ⓐ the ocean
- Ⓑ climates in the United States
- Ⓒ how earthquakes happen
- Ⓓ the best places to go on vacation

_____ **4 What is another name for a *reverse fault*?**

- Ⓐ thrust fault
- Ⓑ strike-slip fault
- Ⓒ normal fault
- Ⓓ San Andreas Fault

_____ **5 What is the effect of too much stress on a fault line?**

- Ⓐ a volcano
- Ⓑ a fault
- Ⓒ an earthquake
- Ⓓ Earth's crust

_____ **6 People who live in __________ are probably very familiar with earthquakes.**

- Ⓐ New York
- Ⓑ California
- Ⓒ London
- Ⓓ Paris

Word Power

Choose the English word from the Vocabulary list that correctly matches the definition.

1 the border between pieces of Earth's crust

____

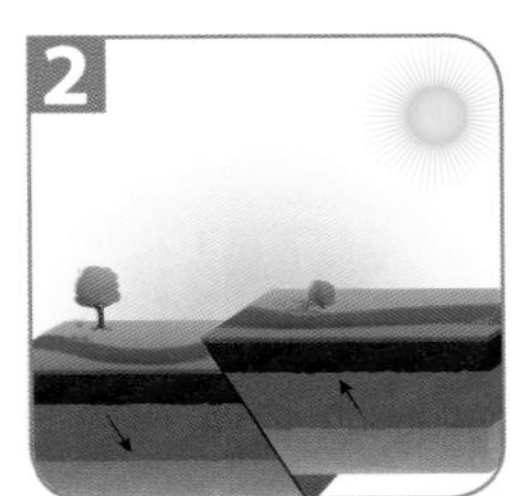

2 two pieces of Earth's crust that are pushing toward each other, causing one piece to move up and over the other

____

3 pressure on an object

____

4 to move or change from one position or direction to another

____

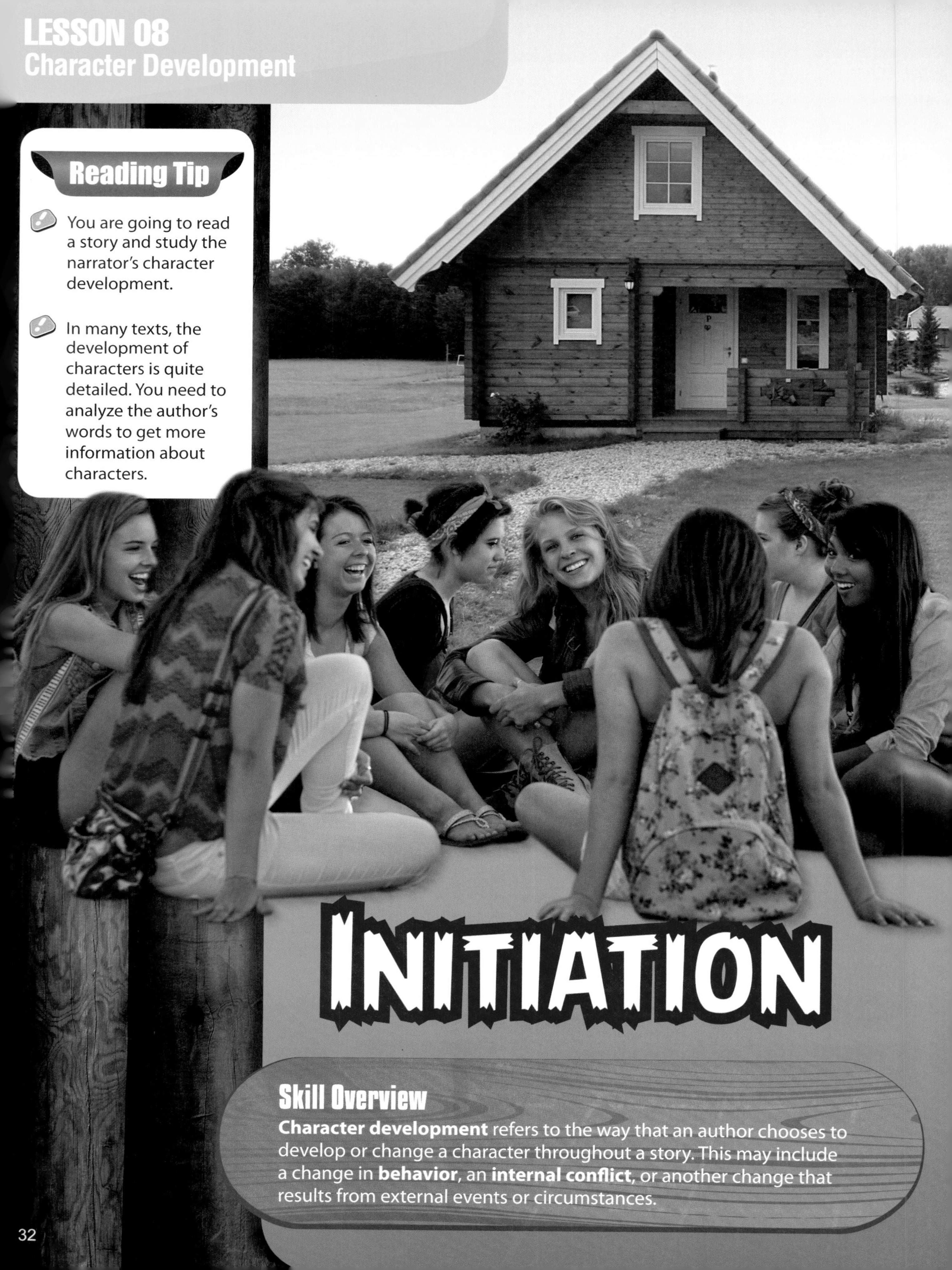

Reading Tip

- You are going to read a story and study the narrator's character development.
- In many texts, the development of characters is quite detailed. You need to analyze the author's words to get more information about characters.

INITIATION

Skill Overview

Character development refers to the way that an author chooses to develop or change a character throughout a story. This may include a change in **behavior**, an **internal conflict**, or another change that results from external events or circumstances.

It was supposed to be a dream come true. A group of popular girls at camp pull me into their cabin and ask me to be "one of them." I dare ask myself, "Why?" After all, I'm neither ugly nor pretty but in that in-between-place of braces and pimples, hair that goes every way but the right way, and clothes that are either too tight or falling off. I'm not a brain, but I'm no dummy. I'm as close to **average** as you can get. Why would the most popular girls at camp seek me out to become one of them? Remember, I'm no dummy.

The girls go on and on about how beautiful, smart, fun, and adventurous I am. "Wow, they must really like me!" I think to myself. That inner voice **exclaiming**, "Warning! Danger!" is crunched because these are **statements** that average people like me never hear.

Each girl takes a turn buttering me up, and then they tell me what an asset I'd be to their "club." The inner voice tries to sneak out, but I **ignore** it. I've always wanted to be wanted, to be accepted, to be liked and admired, to be popular—just like these eight girls.

"So, will you join us?" the leader asks. I nod without a hint of **hesitation**. Giggles should warn me, but I take them as giggles of happiness.

"Well, first, you have to pass the test," one girl announces. I want to inquire why I need to take a test if I'm so wonderful, but I **refrain**. How difficult could the test be? The first question is easy: Who is Letitia?

"She's my best friend," I answer confidently.

"Well, she isn't exactly," the tall girl pauses slightly, "one of us." She continues, "Are you sure she's your best friend?"

"Yeah, I mean, sure," I mutter. "Sometimes." The back of my neck itches, and my sandals feel slippery as I **contemplate** my response. "No, I mean...I guess not," I choke out.

Suddenly, Letitia throws off a sleeping bag and jumps down from the top bunk. I feel empty inside. My heart and mind spin uncontrollably as my eyes fill with fear. Letitia stumbles out of the cabin amidst laughter and **haughty** cries of "Did you see her face?" I meet eight pairs of eyes with a look I can't even explain, a look that penetrates with that voice that wanted to tell me what to do. I exit Cabin 12 and sprint up the dirt path to Cabin 3, where I hope to fix what is now broken.

Vocabulary

average
typical and usual

exclaim
to say or shout something suddenly because of surprise, fear, pleasure, etc.

statement
something that someone says or writes officially

ignore
to intentionally not listen or pay attention to

hesitation
the act of pausing before doing something

✪**refrain**
to keep yourself from doing something

contemplate
to seriously think about something

✪**haughty**
proud and stuck-up

Reading Skill Comprehension Practice

There are different ways for authors to develop their characters. One way is by **traits**, the other is by **motivation**.

A **trait** includes any feature, characteristic, or quality that a person has that makes them unique. It may be a physical trait, or it may be a personality trait.

A **motivation** is a reason for doing something or behaving in a certain way. The motivations of characters often tell us a lot about them.

Record the character traits of the narrator of this passage.

Part 2 **Answer the questions below.**

1. What is the narrator's motivation in this story?
The motivation of the narrator is ______

2. What might be Letitia's motivation?
The motivation of Letitia is ______

3. What is the motivation of the group of popular girls?
The motivation of the group of popular girls is ______

Explain how the narrator changed from the beginning of the story to the end.

______

______

______

______

Comprehension Review

Fill in the best answer for each question.

_____ **1 Which word *best* describes the narrator?**

- A average
- B popular
- C bossy
- D beautiful

_____ **2 The narrator wishes that she were more ___________**

- A athletic.
- B popular.
- C brainy.
- D relaxed.

_____ **3 At the end of the story, the narrator discovers that ___________ is very important to her.**

- A beauty
- B real friendship
- C being popular
- D being admired

_____ **4 *Each girl takes a turn buttering me up...* What does *buttering up* mean in this sentence?**

- A spreading with butter
- B lifting someone up
- C making a promise
- D praising someone to get something in return

_____ **5 At the end of the story, what has been broken?**

- A the narrator's leg
- B a cabin
- C the narrator's friendship with Letitia
- D a bunk bed

_____ **6 What will the narrator probably do when she finds Letitia?**

- A invite her to join the popular girls
- B say that she is sorry
- C invite Letitia to go swimming
- D yell at Letitia

Word Power

Choose the English word from the Vocabulary list that correctly matches the definition.

1

proud and stuck-up

____

2

to keep yourself from doing something

____

3

to seriously think about something

____

4

to intentionally not listen or pay attention to

____

Reading Tip

You will read a short passage about Marie Curie. This passage is an example of a text written in sequential order.

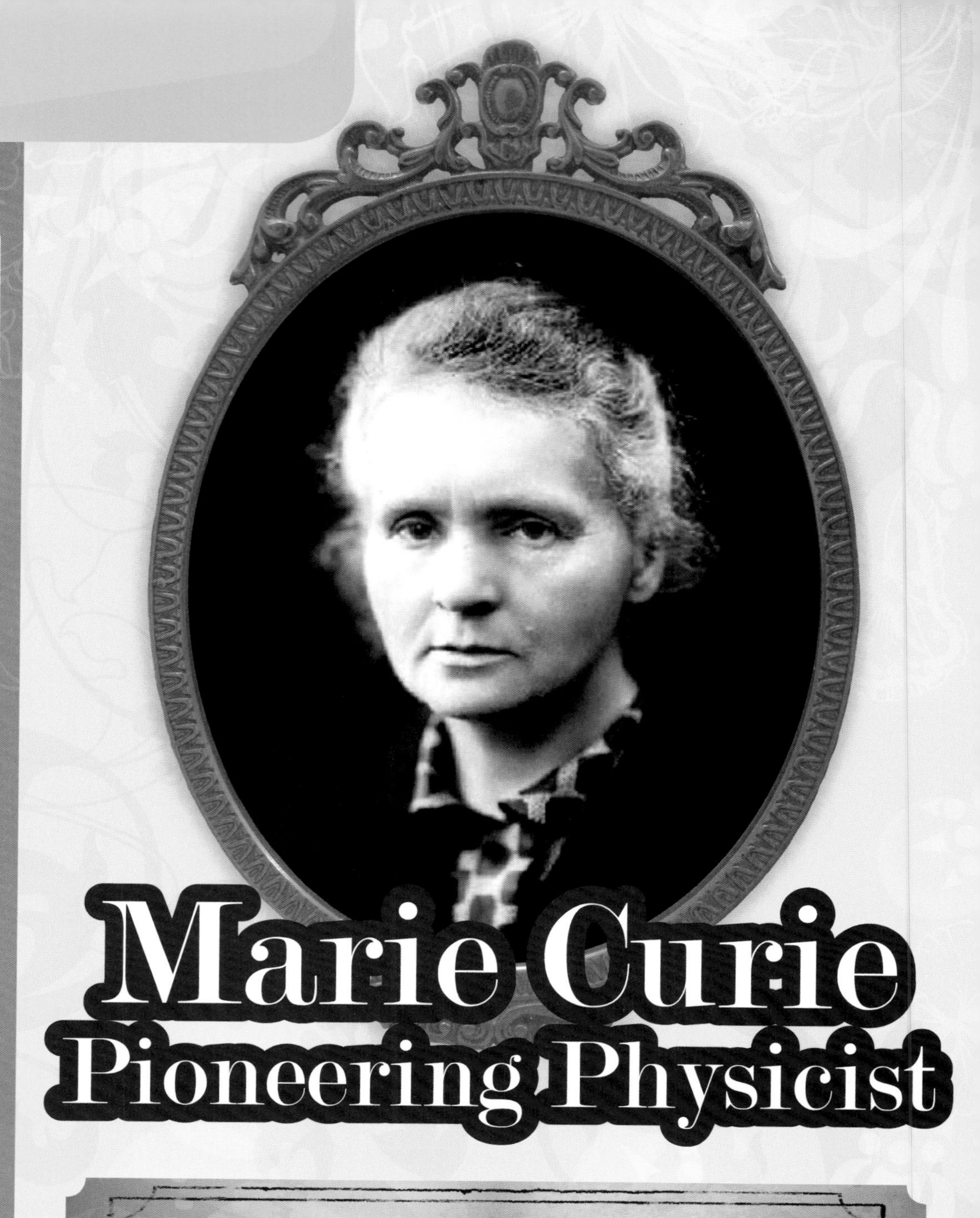

Marie Curie
Pioneering Physicist

Skill Overview

Authors structure their writing so that readers can easily understand the information. Text that is written in sequential order tells the time order in which a process or series of events occurred.

Marie Curie is one of the most important scientists of all time. She spent her life studying energy called ***radiation***. In fact, she invented the word *radioactive* to describe this energy. Her work helped other scientists understand how **atoms** work. Curie also learned many things that led to new ways to **treat** cancer.

Marie Curie (far left) with her father and sisters

The Girl From Poland

Marie Curie was born Marie Sklodowska in Poland on November 7, 1867. Her father was a high school science teacher. Her mother was the principal of a private school for girls. Curie was a good student. Her favorite subjects were science and language arts. She graduated from high school at age 15. She wanted to keep going to school. At that time, however, Polish girls were not allowed to go to college. Soon, Curie and her sister started studying at a secret school. Then they made plans to travel to Paris, France. In 1891, she took the train to Paris.

Studying in Paris

Curie studied at the University of Paris. This university is also called *Sorbonne*. During this time, she lived alone in a small, drafty attic. She loved her classes but had trouble with math. In science, she studied **chemistry** and **physics**. She studied late nearly every night.

Sorbonne

An Important Scientist

Marie Curie was the first woman to win the Nobel Prize. This is the world's highest award for science. She was **awarded** this honor in 1903 for her work in physics. Her work was so successful that she won a second Nobel Prize in 1911 for chemistry. It was for the discovery of radium and polonium. Radium was accepted as a new element. It was later used around the world to treat cancer.

Curie was known as a hard worker and a **brilliant** scientist. She would not stop working until she found answers to her questions. Her tireless work with radiation was important, but it was also dangerous. Too much **exposure** to radiation and radioactive materials made her ill. Sadly, she eventually died from cancer of the blood. Curie will be long remembered for her discoveries in the field of science.

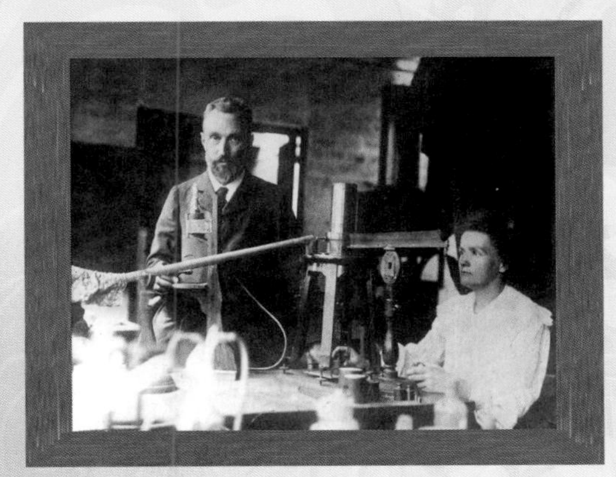

Marie Curie in the laboratory with her husband

Vocabulary

radiation
a form of energy that is sent out in waves or very small particles

atom
the smallest unit of any chemical element

treat
to cure or deal with a disease or injury to make someone feel better

chemistry
the basic characteristics of substances and the different ways in which they react or combine with other substances

physics
the scientific study of matter and energy and the effect that they have on each other

award
to give money or a prize after an official decision

brilliant
extremely intelligent

exposure
state of being unprotected from something dangerous

1911 Nobel Prize diploma

Reading Skill Comprehension Practice

Tell why the author likely wrote this passage in sequential order.

I think the author wrote the passage in sequential order because

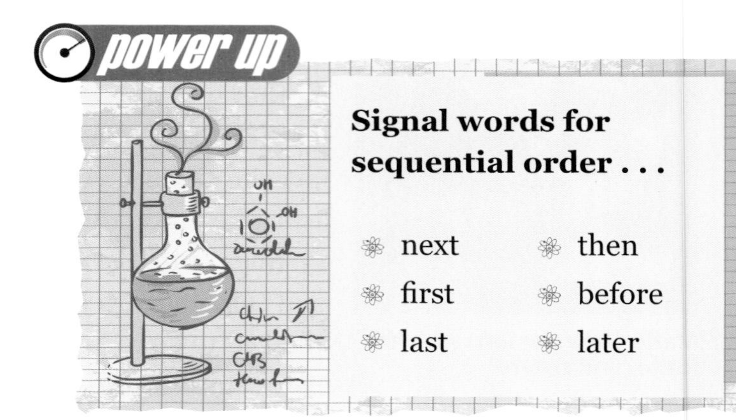

Find two sentences in the passage that contain sequential details. Write the sentences below.

Example 1:

Example 2:

Reread the passage and record any words or phrases that tell the reader that the passage is written in sequential order.

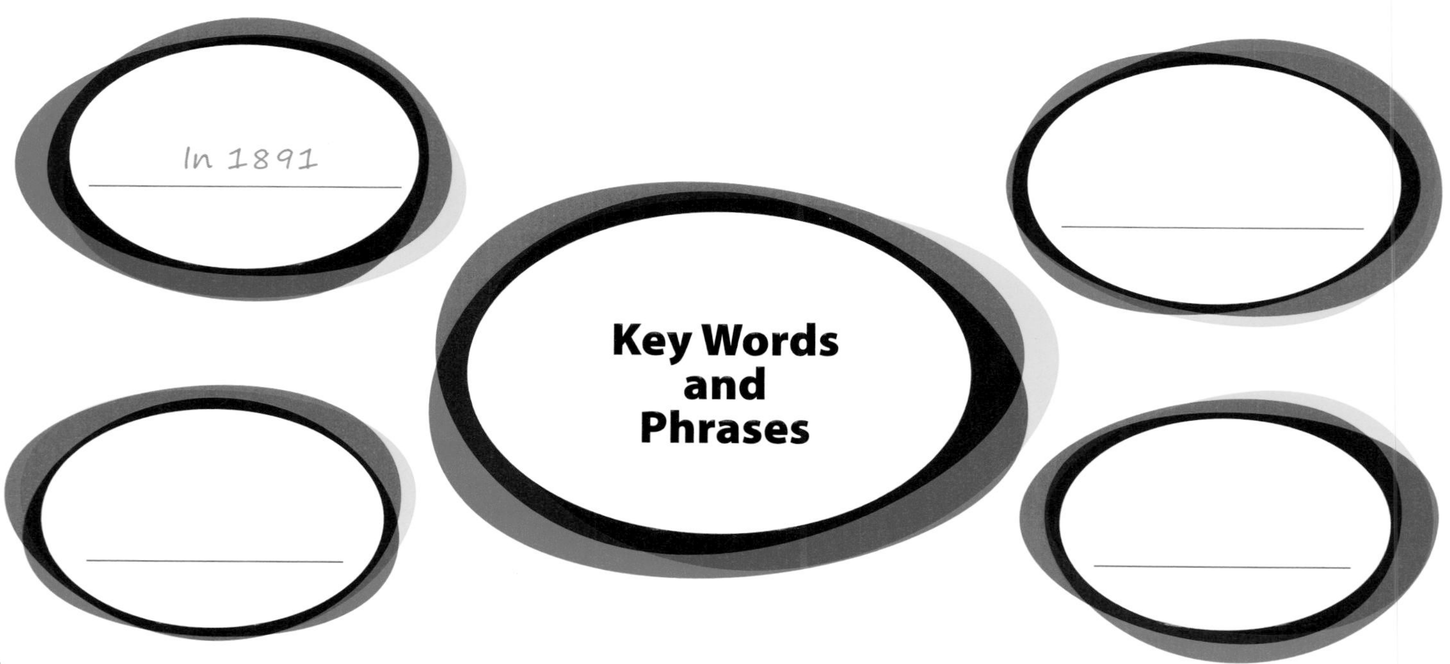

Comprehension Review

Fill in the best answer for each question.

_____ **1 Marie Curie won the Nobel Prize in chemistry ___________**

- Ⓐ before her Nobel Prize in physics.
- Ⓑ before she studied at the secret school with her sister.
- Ⓒ during her time at Sorbonne.
- Ⓓ after her Nobel Prize in physics.

_____ **2 The *first* thing Curie did after she graduated from high school was _____**

- Ⓐ discover radium and polonium.
- Ⓑ study at Sorbonne.
- Ⓒ travel to Paris.
- Ⓓ study at a secret school with her sister.

_____ **3 What is the *last* discovery that Curie made before she died?**

- Ⓐ radium and polonium
- Ⓑ how atoms work
- Ⓒ radiation
- Ⓓ a cure for cancer

_____ **4 Why did Curie travel to Paris for school?**

- Ⓐ Paris was her favorite city.
- Ⓑ Girls were not allowed to go to college in Poland.
- Ⓒ She was offered a scholarship.
- Ⓓ Her family sent her there to be educated.

_____ **5 Which words *best* describe Curie?**

- Ⓐ stubborn and persistent
- Ⓑ lazy and unmotivated
- Ⓒ peaceful and shy
- Ⓓ hardworking and intelligent

_____ **6 Which is *not* true about Curie?**

- Ⓐ She discovered radium and polonium.
- Ⓑ She loved her classes at Sorbonne.
- Ⓒ Her favorite subjects were science and math.
- Ⓓ She was the first woman to receive the Nobel Prize.

Word Power

Choose the English word from the Vocabulary list that correctly matches the definition.

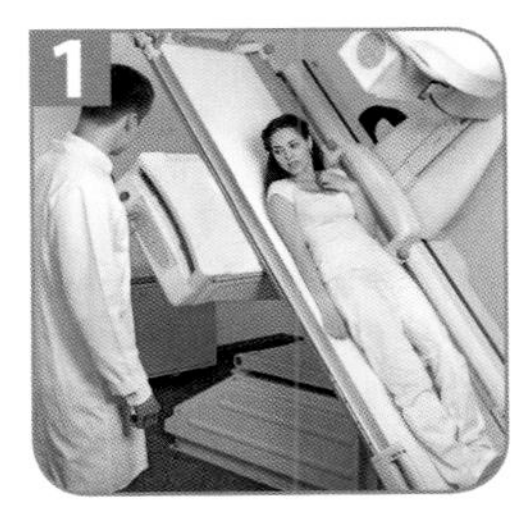

1 state of being unprotected from something dangerous

____

2 extremely intelligent

____

3 a form of energy that is sent out in waves or very small particles

____

4 to give money or a prize after an official decision

____

Reading Tip

Why do authors include headings? How do headings help readers understand a text? Please follow the instructions in Parts 1 to 3 before you listen to and read the passage.

Confucius
Chinese Philosopher

Skill Overview

Headings help a reader **determine the main idea** and to **locate information** in a text. Often, headings state a main idea in a single word or a short phrase and inform the reader about the kind of information contained in the subsequent text.

10

Confucius was a man who lived long ago in China. He grew up during a time of war and chaos. In spite of this, the Chinese made great advances during this time.

Great thinkers called ***philosophers*** wondered about their laws. They questioned, "Is this really right?" They asked others question, too. Because of this, the Chinese gained new ideas about how to live. Confucius was one of these thinkers. He changed Chinese culture. His teachings have **influenced** people for a long time and continue to do so today

Choosing the Right Path

China's history **fascinated** Confucius. He read many books about China that helped him think of ways his government could be better. When the Zhou Dynasty ended, Confucius watched things fall apart. He saw how the poor lived and watched their harvests fail. He saw the government abuse its power. Confucius wanted to help those in need, and he wanted to end wars and fighting. So he **devoted** his life to this cause.

Scholar and Teacher

Confucius decided to start a school. He invited both **nobles** and **peasants** to learn. This was unheard of back then. The people thought that only nobles could be educated. But Confucius knew that schooling would make people equal. He only asked one thing of his students: they had to love learning. He taught his students that the government should help everyone have better lives. He told his students to speak out against dishonest rulers. Because he spoke his mind, many rulers did not like him.

The Greatest Chinese Thinker

China would not be what it is today without Confucius's teachings. Even though some of the original teachings were lost over the years, the basic ideas still exist.

Confucius thought a moral and just society came from two things: education and hard work. He knew that people were smart enough to think for themselves. They should be **valued** for what they could do for their society. He wanted people to use honest language. Confucius also believed that rulers should earn their titles. They should be **virtuous** people who share power.

Looking back, we can see that others have followed these ideas. If Confucius were alive today, he would be amazed. He died thinking that he had not changed China. In truth, Confucius's honest language changed the world.

Vocabulary

philosopher
thinkers; scholars

influence
to cause others to change as a result of one's own actions

fascinate
to interest someone a lot

devote
to give all of something

noble
a person of the highest social group in some countries

peasant
a person who is not well educated or is rude and does not behave well

value
considered important

✪**virtuous**
having a moral or good character

Reading Skill Comprehension Practice

Part 1 Describe a time when you used headings to help you read.

I had used headings to help me read "American School Textbook: Reading and Writing." *It was very useful!*

___

___

___

Explain why an author might include headings in a story or a book.

An author might include headings to

___

___

Use the headings to determine what the passage will be about.
Write your ideas below.

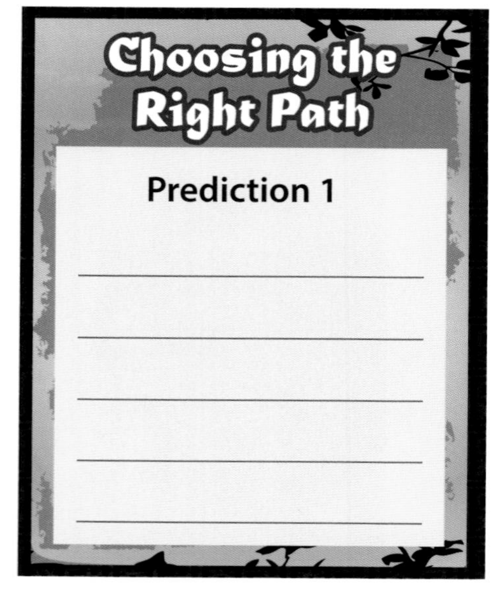

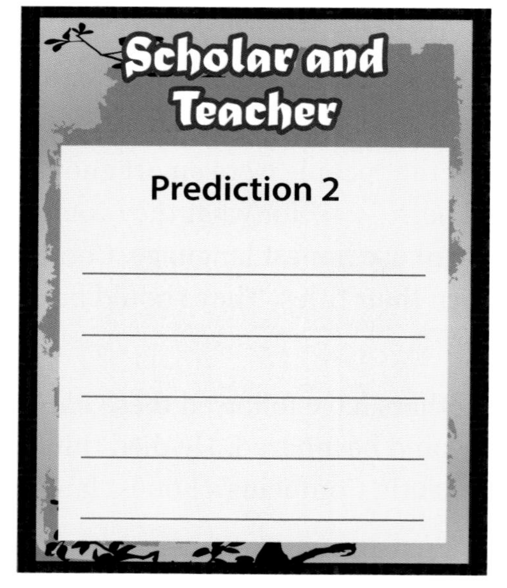

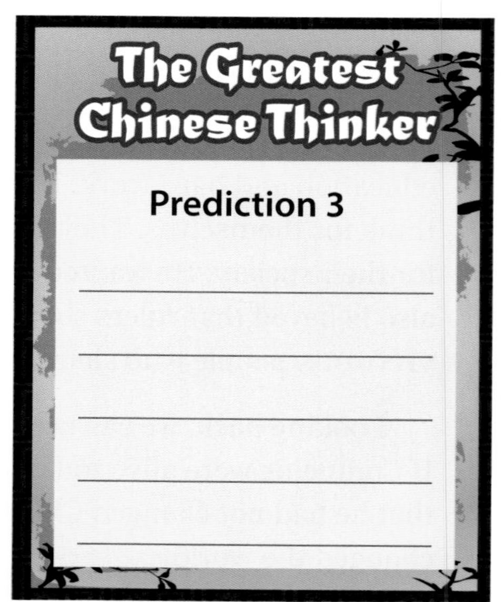

Comprehension Review

Fill in the best answer for each question.

_____ **1** ***"Choosing the Right Path"***
What do you learn about Confucius in this section?

- Ⓐ He lived long ago in China during war and chaos.
- Ⓑ He devoted his life to helping those in need and ending wars.
- Ⓒ He decided to start a new school.
- Ⓓ He told students to speak out against dishonest rulers.

_____ **2** ***"Scholar and Teacher"***
What do you learn about Confucius in this section?

- Ⓐ He was fascinated by China's history.
- Ⓑ He changed Chinese culture.
- Ⓒ He thought that both nobles and peasants should be educated.
- Ⓓ He believed in a moral and just society.

_____ **3** **What would be another good heading for *"The Greatest Chinese Thinker"*?**

- Ⓐ The Great Teachings of Confucius
- Ⓑ Education and Hard Work
- Ⓒ Using Honest Language
- Ⓓ Other Philosophers

_____ **4** **What is the one thing Confucius asked of his students?**

- Ⓐ They had to follow his beliefs.
- Ⓑ They had to revolt against the government.
- Ⓒ They had to use honest language.
- Ⓓ They had to love learning.

_____ **5** **Which is *not* a belief that Confucius held?**

- Ⓐ Rulers should earn their titles.
- Ⓑ Only peasants should be educated.
- Ⓒ The government should help everyone have better lives.
- D People are smart enough to think for themselves.

_____ **6** **Which words *best* describe Confucius?**

- Ⓐ honest and fair
- Ⓑ shy and humble
- Ⓒ rich and powerful
- Ⓓ intelligent and arrogant

Word Power

Choose the English word from the Vocabulary list that correctly matches the definition.

having a moral or good character

____

to give all of something

____

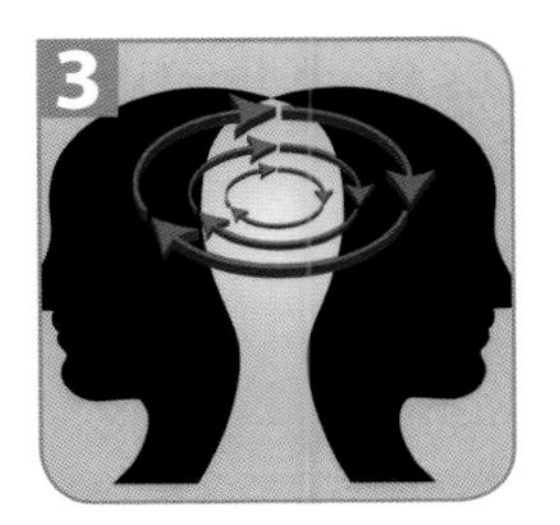

to cause others to change as a result of one's own actions

____

thinkers; scholars

____

Skill Overview

A **topic sentence** introduces and summarizes information to be covered in a passage. Effective readers are able to use topic sentences to make predictions about the upcoming information in the text.

GRAVITY

When you walk around, you are "stuck" to the ground. You can jump, but the ground always gets you in the end. Why is this?

Isaac Newton was the first to **realize** that the **force** that makes planets go around the Sun is the same force that makes things fall to Earth. It is called ***gravity***. A story about Newton says that he figured out gravity when he saw an apple fall from a tree. He realized that the apple and the Moon are similar. Gravity attracts them both to Earth.

Gravity is what holds us on the ground and keeps us from floating into space. It also keeps Earth going around the Sun and the Moon going around Earth. Without gravity, things would just bob in space. Everyday life would be difficult.

Reading Tip

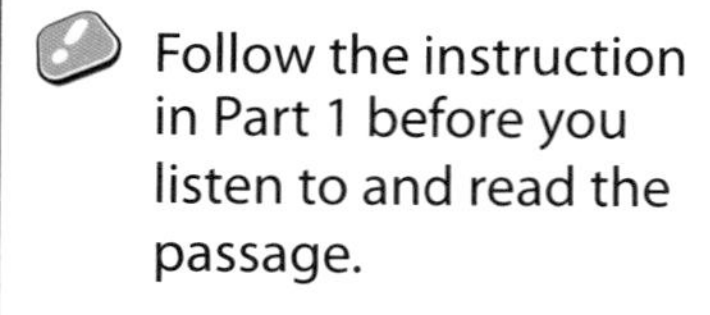

- Follow the instruction in Part 1 before you listen to and read the passage.

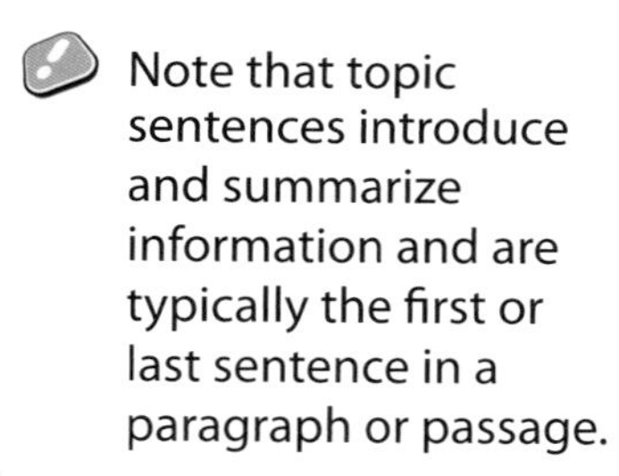

- Note that topic sentences introduce and summarize information and are typically the first or last sentence in a paragraph or passage.

BIG GRAVITY

Watching the planets in the sky, Newton figured out that they were pulled toward the Sun. The closer the planets were to the Sun, the stronger the pull on them.

He also watched the Moon. He knew that the Moon was moving around Earth. But why did its path curve around instead of shooting away from Earth in a straight line? This was Newton's First Law of Motion: Objects continue moving in the same direction unless another force makes them change **direction**.

Newton figured out what must be changing the Moon's direction: Earth's gravity. Earth's gravity gives it a **constant** tug, which pulls it around in a circle. Think of a ball on a string. If you swing the ball around your head, the **tension** in the string is like gravity. It keeps the ball moving in a circle. If you were to let go of the string, the ball would fly off at an angle. This is what would happen to the Moon if Earth's gravity stopped working.

The reason Earth's gravity doesn't make the Moon fall down and land on Earth is that the Moon has energy from its motion. If something came along that stopped the Moon from moving, it would start falling toward Earth. Just as in the ball example, letting the ball slow down too much makes it collapse toward you!

Vocabulary

realize
to understand a situation

force
physical, especially violent, strength or power

gravity
the force that causes things to fall toward Earth

direction
the position toward which someone or something moves or faces

constant
happening without stopping

tension
the degree to which something is stretched

universe
all of the stars, planets, and other objects in space

exert
to use something, such as power, in order to make something happen

LITTLE GRAVITY

Everything in the **universe exerts** a pull of gravity on everything else. The strength of that pull is determined by the object's mass and how far away it is. A heavy object has a big pull of gravity. A faraway object has a smaller pull of gravity. The heaviest, closest thing to you right now is Earth. Because it's heavy and close, you feel its pull the strongest.

You can't feel it, but you have gravity, too. You have mass, so you have gravity. However, compared to Earth, your gravity is not very strong. If you were floating out in space, though, you could have your own Moon orbiting around you—maybe your little sister!

Reading Skill Comprehension Practice

Part 1 Read the topic sentence from the passage below, and use it to predict what the passage will be about.

Topic Sentence

Gravity is what holds us on the ground and keeps us from floating into space.

My Prediction

____

____

Part 2 After reading "Gravity," use the space below to describe what the passage is actually about.

What the Passage Is About

____

____

Part 3 Find other topic sentences in the passage, and write them below.

1. *Newton figured out what must be changing the Moon's direction: Earth's gravity.*
2. ______________________________
3. ______________________________

Comprehension Review

Fill in the best answer for each question.

_____ **1 Which of these is the topic sentence that tells the main idea of the passage?**

Ⓐ You can jump, but the ground always gets you in the end.
Ⓑ Gravity attracts them both to Earth.
Ⓒ It also keeps Earth going around the Sun and the Moon going around Earth.
Ⓓ Gravity is what holds us on the ground and keeps us from floating into space.

_____ **2 *Newton figured out what must be changing the Moon's direction: Earth's gravity.***
This topic sentence tells you that the paragraph will be about _____

Ⓐ Newton's Second Law of Motion.
Ⓑ Moon landings.
Ⓒ how Earth's gravity affects other objects in the solar system.
Ⓓ the planets of our solar system.

_____ **3 *Everything in the universe exerts a pull of gravity on everything else.***
What can you predict from this topic sentence?

Ⓐ Earth does not exert gravity.
Ⓑ The Moon exerts a pull of gravity.
Ⓒ Earth's gravity does not affect you.
Ⓓ The Sun is not in the universe.

_____ **4 Where would you probably find a passage like this?**

Ⓐ a science fiction novel
Ⓑ an instruction manual
Ⓒ a science book
Ⓓ a book of poetry

_____ **5 The closer something is, _____**

Ⓐ the stronger its pull of gravity.
Ⓑ the weaker its pull of gravity.
Ⓒ the smaller it is.
Ⓓ the harder it is to see.

_____ **6 How are an apple and the Moon similar?**

Ⓐ They both fall to Earth.
Ⓑ Earth's gravity attracts both of them.
Ⓒ They are both too far away to see without a telescope.
Ⓓ They both float in space.

Word Power

Choose the English word from the Vocabulary list that correctly matches the definition.

1

all of the stars, planets, and other objects in space

____

2

happening without stopping

____

3

the force that causes things to fall toward Earth

____

4

physical, especially violent, strength or power

____

Toss Me a Line!

Reading Tip

Listen to and read the first two paragraphs, and then follow the instructions in Parts 1 and 2.

Mame
Tonight, 7 p.m.

Skill Overview

Literary devices are specific aspects of writing that help readers understand a given text. These include **personification**, **simile**, **metaphor**, **alliteration**, **tone**, **flashback**, **foreshadowing**, and **suspense**.

12

It's one of those **horrors** you hear people talk about. You're on **stage** in the middle of a **play**, but you can't remember your lines. Unfortunately for me, this was not a nightmare—this was real. I stood frozen on the long stairway of the set for the musical *Mame*.

That afternoon, Mrs. Hollingsworth, our middle school drama teacher, had sprinted up to me—a **clumsy** linebacker on the school football team. Her crazy hair was standing straight up like cobras reacting to a snake charmer's music. She shouted at me, "One of my actors is out sick! He has just one line and you're the only one who fits his **costume**!"

I felt sorry for her and said, "Okay." I mumbled something about how the show must go on.

"You won't **regret** your decision!" she announced. But now, in the middle of the performance, I think no one regretted my decision more than she did. On stage, I opened my mouth to speak. Nothing came out.

I knew the scene called for a toast. All the actors had raised their glasses full of orange juice. Whatever I was supposed to say, I couldn't tell you if my life depended on it. Not only had I forgotten my line, but I also couldn't breathe, swallow, or even blink. And that's not good if you wear contact lenses.

Doink! The contact lens popped out of my left eye and whizzed toward the audience. In one motion, I tossed aside my glass of orange juice—barely noticing the orange juice splatter the guy next to me—and plucked the flying lens out of the tension-filled air.

In the process, my arm accidentally pushed against Andrea Rotelli, the girl playing Mame. She lost her balance and stumbled down the stairway. Sure, she lost a shoe that banged down the steps like a sack of rocks. But she was good. By the end of the stumble, she managed to turn her movements into a little disco-like dance. In that moment of panic, all I could wonder was how to keep my contact lens moist so it didn't crumble.

Without thinking, I stepped down to Andrea. I snatched the glass out of her hand and plopped the contact lens in it. She gave me a look that would have driven Sir Laurence Olivier from the stage, screaming in terror.

"Darling," she hissed at me, a fake smile plastered on her face. "You're such a silly! I want to give a toast!" She grabbed her glass back. "To life!" she screamed quickly, worried I'd **interrupt** again. And then she drank the juice from the cup. All of it, including my contact lens, was long gone.

No one was happier than I was—with the possible **exceptions** of Andrea and Mrs. Hollingsworth—when I returned to the football field. In football, the only lines I had to remember were "Grrr!" and "Get out of my way!"

Vocabulary

horror
something that is very shocking or frightening

stage
the area in a theater that is often raised above ground level and on which actors or entertainers perform

play
a story that is acted out on a stage

clumsy
awkward

costume
a set of clothes suitable for a particular activity

regret
to feel bad and wish that you had not done something

interrupt
to stop a person from speaking for a short period by saying or doing something

exception
a case in which normal rules do not apply

Reading Skill Comprehension Practice

Suspense
(first paragraph)

It makes readers feel excitement and uncertainty about what will happen in a story. It also makes readers want to read on and find out what happens.

Foreshadowing
(first paragraph)

It is a technique an author uses to indicate or suggest something that is going to happen in a story.

Flashback
(passage)

This is a plot point from the past that appears out of chronological order in a story.

Part 1 After reading the first paragraph, write your thoughts and predictions about the **suspenseful moment** described in the first three sentences.

____

____

____

Part 2 Explain how the author uses **foreshadowing** in the second paragraph.

____

____

____

Part 3 Explain how a **flashback** is used in the passage. Tell how this makes the passage more interesting.

____

____

____

Comprehension Review

Fill in the best answer for each question.

_____ ❶ ***Her crazy hair was standing straight up like cobras reacting to a snake charmer's music.***

This is an example of __________

- Ⓐ a metaphor.
- Ⓑ rhyming.
- Ⓒ alliteration.
- Ⓓ a simile.

_____ ❷ **Which one is an example of onomatopoeia*?**

- Ⓐ whizzed
- Ⓑ a shoe that dropped down the steps like a sack of rocks
- Ⓒ I stood frozen
- Ⓓ glass of grape juice

_____ ❸ ***...and plucked the flying lens out of the tension-filled air.***

In this sentence, *plucked* means __________

- Ⓐ stuck.
- Ⓑ smeared.
- Ⓒ grabbed.
- Ⓓ pulled out.

_____ ❹ **You can infer that the narrator is __________**

- Ⓐ a girl.
- Ⓑ a boy.
- Ⓒ an adult.
- Ⓓ an actor.

_____ ❺ **Which sentence describes a problem in the story?**

- Ⓐ The narrator is on the football team.
- Ⓑ Andrea Rotelli is playing Mame.
- Ⓒ Mrs. Hollingsworth is the high school drama teacher.
- Ⓓ The narrator forgot his line.

_____ ❻ **What is Mrs. Hollingsworth's solution to her problem?**

- Ⓐ She asks the narrator to take the place of an actor.
- Ⓑ She asks Andrea Rotelli to take the place of another actor.
- Ⓒ She plops her contact lens into a glass of orange juice.
- Ⓓ She writes a new play.

onomatopoeia*
words created to imitate a natural sound or to sound like the thing being described

Word Power

Choose the English word from the Vocabulary list that correctly matches the definition.

1 awkward

____

2 a case in which normal rules do not apply

____

3 to feel bad and wish that you had not done something

____

4 the area in a theater that is often raised above ground level and on which actors or entertainers perform

____

LESSON 13
Cause and Effect

Dancing Masai women

AFRICAN HISTORY

Reading Tip

You can often recognize a cause-and-effect pattern in a text by the use of signal words or phrases.

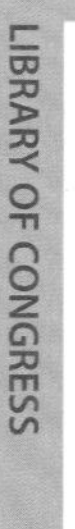

The Kush carrying ivory tusks

Skill Overview

Cause and effect is a pattern in text that explains the result of an event or occurrence and the reasons it happened. Successful readers identify cause-and-effect structure and use appropriate strategies to better understand the text.

Africa is the second-largest continent. It is bigger than the United States and Europe combined. Africa lies south of Europe and southwest of the Middle East.

Trading goods made the African cultures rich. When **empires** gained control of trade **routes**, their power grew. When they lost **control** of these routes, they lost their power and **wealth**.

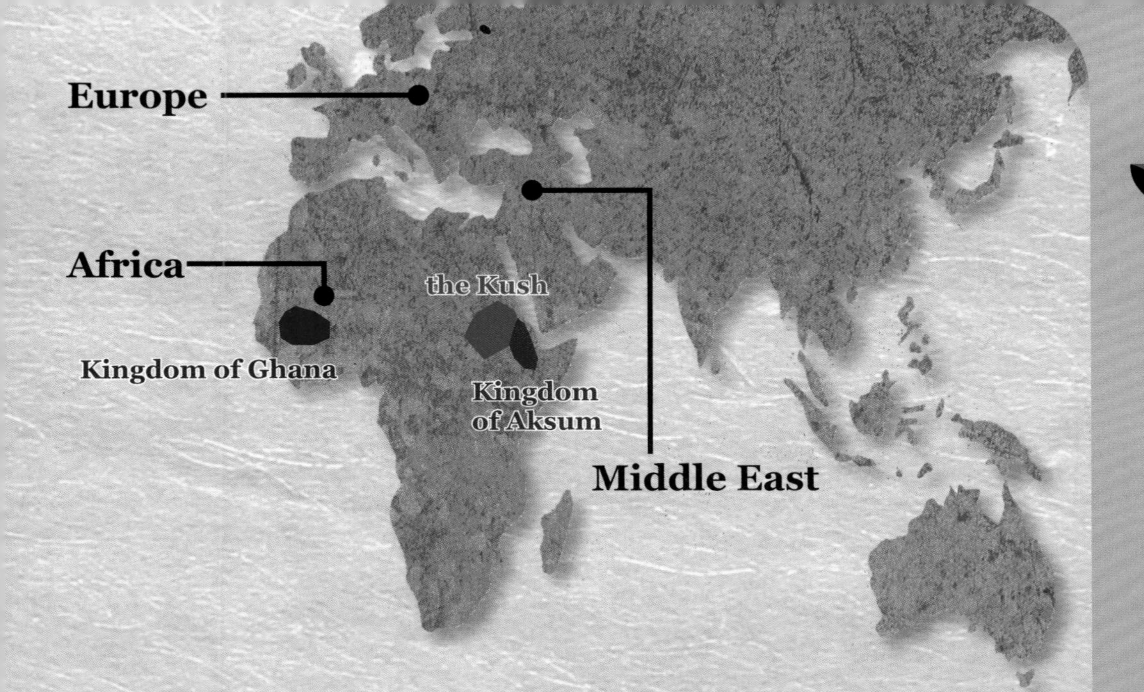

THE KUSH AND THE KINGDOM OF AKSUM

The Kush had one of the first **civilizations** in Africa, ruling what is now the country of Sudan. They made tools and weapons of iron. Egyptian **trade** routes passed through the Kush kingdom. People carried ivory, ebony, and animal furs on these routes. Since the Kush owned these routes, they charged fees to use them. As a result, the Kush became rich.

The **kingdom** of Aksum rose to power in the first century A.D. The Aksum people traded crops, gold, and ivory along the coast of the Red Sea. Merchants going to the East passed through Aksum's **port** city on the Red Sea. Because of this, the Aksum rulers had a connection to India, Egypt, and the Roman Empire. This brought the Aksum rulers great wealth. Around A.D. 700, Arabs took control of all these trade routes. Therefore, the Aksum people lost their power.

THE EMPIRE OF GHANA

The prophet Muhammad began the religion of Islam around A.D. 600. His followers are called *Muslims*. In the 700s, Muslim traders started to trade gold. They traveled from North Africa to West Africa by moving through the Empire of Ghana. West Africans needed a way to keep their food from spoiling. Salt preserved food and made it safe to eat, but West Africans could not make their own salt. They had gold mines, so the Muslims traded salt for gold. Most of the world's gold came from West Africa.

Ghana owned the major trade routes in northwest Africa. At one point, the Muslims tried to force the people of Ghana to change religions. This led to fighting, which made the empire weaker. Then North Africans attacked Ghana and seized the trade routes. By 1203, Ghana had been taken over.

Vocabulary

empire
a group of countries or regions controlled by a single government or ruler

route
path of travel

control
to limit or rule over something or over someone's actions or behaviors

wealth
money and possessions that have value

civilization
human society with its well-developed social organizations

trade
the activity of buying and selling, or exchanging, goods

kingdom
an area that is controlled by a particular person

port
a town by the sea or by a river that has a harbor

Gold

Salt

Reading Skill Comprehension Practice

Part 1 List the words or phrases in the passage that made you realize it is written in a cause-and-effect pattern.

so

Part 2 Record at least one example of cause and effect in the passage.

1. Since the Kush owned these routes, they charged fees to use them.

2. ______

Part 3 Each row in the chart below contains either a cause or an effect; fill in the missing information (e.g., What made it happen? What happened?) in the empty boxes.

	Cause—What made it happen?	Effect—What happened?
1		It made the African cultures rich.
2	Muslims tried to force the people of Ghana to change religions.	
3		The Aksum people lost their power.
4	Egyptian trade routes passed through the Kush kingdom.	
5		The empires' power grew.

Comprehension Review

Fill in the best answer for each question.

_____ **1 What caused the Kush to become rich?**
- Ⓐ They had one of the first civilizations in Africa.
- Ⓑ They charged fees for using their trade routes.
- Ⓒ Expensive goods were brought in from the trade routes.
- Ⓓ They formed an alliance with the kingdom of Aksum.

_____ **2 Which was *not* an effect of the Muslims forcing the people of Ghana to change religions?**
- Ⓐ North Africans attacked Ghana.
- Ⓑ Fighting ensued, and the Empire of Ghana weakened.
- Ⓒ Ghana agreed and formed an alliance with the Muslims.
- Ⓓ The North Africans took control of the trade routes in Ghana.

_____ **3 Why did the Aksum people lose their power?**
- Ⓐ Eventually, the Arabs took control of all their trade routes.
- Ⓑ India, Egypt, and the Roman Empire stopped all trade with the Aksum rulers.
- Ⓒ Merchants stopped passing through their port cities, so they lost business.
- Ⓓ Fighting among the Aksum people caused chaos and unrest.

_____ **4 What produced the most wealth for many African cultures?**
- Ⓐ natural resources on the land
- Ⓑ salt
- Ⓒ trading goods
- Ⓓ powerful rulers

_____ **5 What are followers of the religion of Islam called?**
- Ⓐ North Africans
- Ⓑ Kush
- Ⓒ Hindus
- Ⓓ Muslims

_____ **6 Because the West Africans could not make their own salt, _____**
- Ⓐ they could not preserve food, which caused everyone to get sick.
- Ⓑ they traded gold for salt.
- Ⓒ they traveled to North Africa for salt.
- Ⓓ they took salt from neighboring lands.

Word Power

Choose the English word from the Vocabulary list that correctly matches the definition.

1

money and possessions that have value

____

2

the activity of buying and selling, or exchanging, goods

____

3

path of travel

____

4

a group of countries or regions controlled by a single government or ruler

____

Reading Tip

- Think about how you would paraphrase this passage to someone who has not read the story.
- An important part of paraphrasing is to retell a story **in one's own words**.
- One way to paraphrase information from a passage is to **focus on the main idea**.

Skill Overview

Paraphrasing means retelling information in a text in one's own words. Readers must read carefully and focus on important information in order to retell a passage after reading.

THE SICK LION

14

One day the lion, king of all the **beasts**, was extremely ill. He did not come out of his cave, but instead lay **groaning** and murmuring barely **audible** roars whenever anyone came near.

The other animals did not know what to do. For as long as they could remember, the lion had made all their **decisions**. They had long since forgotten how to think for themselves.

After much discussion, they agreed that they must visit him in his cave, for if they stayed away, he would certainly be angry and they would suffer. Besides, in his current condition, he couldn't harm them.

So one at a time, the animals went to the royal cave. Some took him a gift, such as their best pieces of meat. Others just went to **inquire** about his health. Large and small, each animal in the lion's kingdom made its way to his dwelling. However, the fox stayed away. Eventually, the lion noticed that the fox never visited him. So the king sent his servant, a hyena, to inquire why the fox was being so rude.

"Fox," said the hyena, "you have displeased His Majesty, the lion. Although he is desperately ill, you have not come to ask how he is feeling. What **excuse** do you have for your disrespectful behavior?"

The fox replied, "Hyena, I would like to see the king, for I respect his wisdom. Indeed, I once came right to the mouth of the cave bearing my best piece of meat as a get-well present. Although I was anxious to see the king, when I got there I noticed something that made me too frightened to go in."

"And what was that?" asked the hyena.

The fox replied, "I saw many pairs of footprints in the sand from all sorts of animals. But they were all going one way—into the cave. Not a single footprint came out. I did not want to enter a place from which I would never return."

The clever fox had **figured out** the lion's **devious** plan. Believing he was sick and harmless, the animals he usually chased down for food came right into his cave—ending up as his next meal.

Vocabulary

beast
animal

groan
to make a long, deep sound showing great pain or unhappiness

✪**audible**
able to be heard

decision
a choice that you make about something

inquire
to ask for information

excuse
a reason given to explain some behavior

figure out
to find out

✪**devious**
sneaky or deceptive

Reading Skill Comprehension Practice

Part 1 Answer the questions below.

1. What is paraphrasing?

Paraphrasing is ______________________

____

2. Why is it important for a reader to paraphrase?

____

____

3. Why should readers use their own words when paraphrasing?

____

____

4. What type of information should readers include when they are paraphrasing a text?

____

____

Part 2 Think about which information in this passage is important, and then paraphrase it in your own words.

____

____

____

Part 3 Consider how you can improve your paraphrasing in Part 2.
Use the 5W and H questions (who, what, where, when, why, how) to help you.

____

____

____

____

____

Comprehension Review

Fill in the best answer for each question.

_____ **1 Which sentence best paraphrases the reason the fox did not visit the lion?**

- Ⓐ The fox saw footprints going into the cave but not out, so he knew the animals were being eaten.
- Ⓑ The fox didn't like the lion.
- Ⓒ The fox didn't want to go in the cave with other animals there.
- Ⓓ The fox saw that the hyena was at the cave. He was afraid of the hyena, so he left.

_____ **2 Which event did *not* happen in the story?**

- Ⓐ When the animals found out the lion was sick, they went to visit him.
- Ⓑ The lion asked the hyena to find out why the fox was being rude.
- Ⓒ There were footprints going into the lion's cave, but not coming out.
- Ⓓ The fox and the hyena went to visit the lion.

_____ **3 When you are telling this story to someone else, which event should come *first*?**

- Ⓐ The hyena went to visit the fox.
- Ⓑ The lion appeared to be very sick.
- Ⓒ The animals visited the lion.
- Ⓓ The fox figured out the lion's plan.

_____ **4 *...each animal in the lion's kingdom made its way to his dwelling.***

In this passage, what does the word *dwelling* mean?

- Ⓐ a forest
- Ⓑ a kind of lion
- Ⓒ a cave
- Ⓓ a large animal

_____ **5 Which word *best* describes the fox?**

- Ⓐ lazy
- Ⓑ clever
- Ⓒ stupid
- Ⓓ funny

_____ **6 Why didn't the other animals know what to do when the lion got sick?**

- Ⓐ They did not know what a lion is.
- Ⓑ They could not find the lion.
- Ⓒ They were used to the lion telling them what to do.
- Ⓓ They brought the lion gifts.

Word Power

Choose the English word from the Vocabulary list that correctly matches the definition.

1

able to be heard

____

2

sneaky or deceptive

____

3

animal

____

4

to make a long, deep sound showing great pain or unhappiness

____

Skill Overview

A summary sentence summarizes the information in a passage, usually in the last sentence of a passage or paragraph. Effective readers are able to use summary sentences to determine main ideas and identify the most important information in a text.

My Idol Bad Boy Michaels

Reading Tip

- Listen to and read all but the last paragraph of this passage, and then follow the instruction in Part 1.
- Summary sentences are important because they both **summarize the information** in a story and **extend the author's message** in an interesting way.

15

Leo Garcia was a sixth-grade boy who liked to play baseball. Anytime he wasn't in class or home doing chores, you could find him on the ball **field**. Everyone said that someday Leo would be a famous ballplayer.

Leo's **idol** was a baseball player named Phil Michaels. The sportswriters had nicknamed him "Bad Boy Michaels" because he was always getting into trouble. He was either in a fight or staying out past the team **curfew**. On the field, he argued with the **umpires** or attacked pitchers he thought had tried to hit him with a ball. Leo looked up to Bad Boy as his idol and wanted to be just like him. He even started calling himself "Bad Boy!"

His friends didn't like Leo's new bad-boy image. Like the baseball player, Leo was trying to pick fights with his friends. He started making trouble in class by talking back to the teachers, teasing other students, and getting sent to the principal's office. At home, he was mean to his sisters and brothers and even talked back to his mother when she told him to sit down. Soon, people didn't like Bad Boy Garcia very much.

Vocabulary

field
an area, usually covered with grass, used for playing sports

idol
a person who is greatly admired and loved

✪**curfew**
a time when certain underage persons are required to be home

umpire
a person who is present at a sports competition to make sure that the rules of the game are obeyed

thrilled
extremely pleased

usher
to show someone where they should go

rude
not polite

✪**scram**
to go away

One day, his father asked him if he would like to go to a baseball game. "Phil Michaels is playing. The assistant coach is a friend of mine. He can get us in so you can meet Bad Boy." Leo was **thrilled** to get a chance to meet his idol.

When the big day came, Leo was ready. When they arrived, they went around the back to the team's locker room. His dad's friend **ushered** them into the room where Bad Boy was talking to the press. Listening to the questions and answers, Leo didn't like the way Bad Boy was being mean-tempered and **rude** to all the reporters. Then his dad's friend introduced them to Bad Boy, who said, "Why do you keep bringing these annoying kids around to see me? **Scram**! kid; can't you see I'm busy?" Leo felt like he had been slapped in the face.

Bad Boy Garcia changed his name and his idol after that. He decided that being rude and mean to people—especially kids—was not the kind of ballplayer or person he wanted to be.

Reading Skill Comprehension Practice

Part 1 Think about the characters in this passage. Write your reactions below.

My thoughts about the characters in the passage are . . .

I think the character is . . .

____

____

____

Part 2 Now that you have read the whole passage, answer the questions below.

1. What do you think about the characters now?

____

____

____

____

2. Why is your reaction different from the one you recorded in Part 1?

____

____

____

____

Part 3 Write the author's main idea, or central message, in this passage.

The main idea, or central message, of the passage is that ____

____

____

____

Comprehension Review

Fill in the best answer for each question.

_____ **1 Which sentence is a summary of the second paragraph?**

- Ⓐ He was either in a fight or staying out past the team curfew.
- Ⓑ He even started calling himself "Bad Boy!"
- Ⓒ When the big day came, Leo was ready.
- Ⓓ The sportswriters had nicknamed him "Bad Boy Michaels" because he was always getting into trouble.

_____ **2 *Soon, people didn't like Bad Boy Garcia very much.***

Which detail supports this summary?

- Ⓐ Leo Garcia liked to play baseball.
- Ⓑ Leo started making trouble in class.
- Ⓒ Leo's father asked him if he would like to meet Phil Michaels.
- Ⓓ Leo felt like he had been slapped in the face.

_____ **3 Which sentence summarizes the lesson Leo learned?**

- Ⓐ Leo felt like he had been slapped in the face.
- Ⓑ When the big day came, Leo was ready.
- Ⓒ He decided that being rude and mean to people was not the kind of person he wanted to be.
- Ⓓ Leo saw Bad Boy talking to the press.

_____ **4 Why did Leo begin to make trouble in class?**

- Ⓐ He wanted to be like his idol.
- Ⓑ He failed a big test.
- Ⓒ His best friend dared him to get in trouble.
- Ⓓ He did not like the teacher.

_____ **5 *Leo felt like he had been slapped in the face.***

This caused Leo to _____

- Ⓐ be mean to kids at school.
- Ⓑ stop playing baseball.
- Ⓒ like Bad Boy Michaels even more.
- Ⓓ change his name and idol.

_____ **6 What is the main idea of this story?**

- Ⓐ Baseball is a fun sport.
- Ⓑ Being rude and mean to people is not the best way to act.
- Ⓒ If you work hard and practice, you can meet your idol.
- Ⓓ Most baseball players are very rude, especially to kids.

Word Power

Choose the English word from the Vocabulary list that correctly matches the definition.

1 to go away

____

2 a person who is greatly admired and loved

____

3 extremely pleased

____

4 a time when certain underage persons are required to be home

____

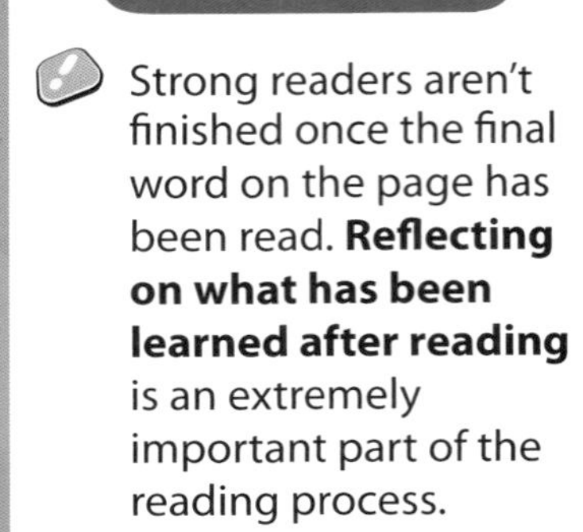

Reading Tip

- Strong readers aren't finished once the final word on the page has been read. **Reflecting on what has been learned after reading** is an extremely important part of the reading process.

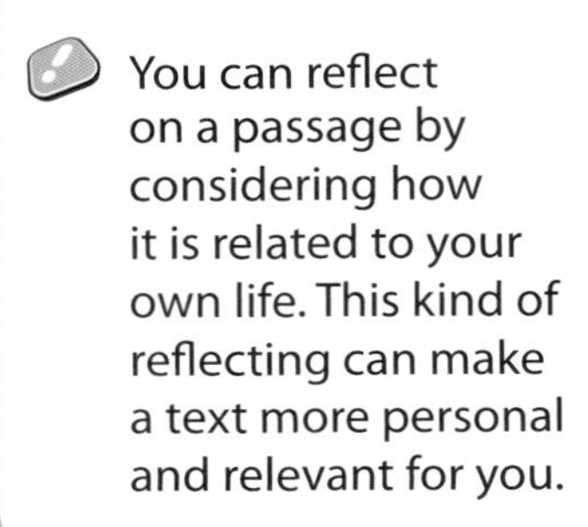

- You can reflect on a passage by considering how it is related to your own life. This kind of reflecting can make a text more personal and relevant for you.

Radiant Light

Skill Overview

Readers reflect on a text when they think about what has been read and form ideas, opinions, or responses. Reflecting helps readers make sense of what they have read and connect it with what they already know.

The energy of light is called *radiant energy*. To ***radiate*** means to send out rays or waves. Only a certain type of radiant energy can be seen with the human eye. We call this ***visible** light*. *Visible* means that we can see it.

We can see because of light. Light waves **bounce** off objects and travel to our eyes. Our eyes and brain work together to translate that light into what we see.

Light travels in waves much like water moves in waves. The amount of energy that a wave carries **determines** the color of the light. Waves differ from one another in length, rate, and size. These are called *wavelength*, *frequency*, and *amplitude*. Frequency **relates** to the color of the light.

Refract, Reflect, Absorb

What happens when a light wave hits the atoms that make up everything? Several things might happen:

- The light can change direction, or refract.
- Some of the light rays can reflect off of the surface.
- The light can be absorbed into the material.

Light rays bend as they travel through the surface of transparent material. If something is transparent, that means light can be seen through it and move through it. This bend in the light is called ***refraction***. It **occurs** when light travels through different materials at different speeds.

The return of a wave of energy after it strikes a surface is called ***reflection***. Smooth and polished surfaces, such as mirrors, reflect more light than surfaces that are rough or bumpy.

When light reflects from a smooth surface, all of the light rays reflect in the same direction. A mirror is smooth, so you can see your image in it. When light reflects off a rough surface, the rays reflect in many directions. It is impossible to see your reflection in paper because the surface is rough.

Reflection

Vocabulary

radiate
to send out rays or waves

visible
able to be seen

bounce
to move up or away after hitting a surface

determine
to control or influence something directly

relate
to find or show the connection between two or more things

✪**refraction**
a bend in a light ray

occur
to happen

reflection
the return of a wave of light

Refraction

Reading Skill Comprehension Practice

Think about the passage you just read. Write down any ideas or opinions you have about the material presented in the passage.

This passage made me think about ______________________________

____

____

____

Consider how this passage is relevant to your life. Write your personal response below.

This passage is relevant to my life because ______________________________

____

____

____

Part 3 Identify other information that could be added to this passage to help readers understand the material.

I think the passage could have included some

examples of ______________________________

____

____

____

____

____

____

Comprehension Review

Fill in the best answer for each question.

_____ **1 According to the passage, which of these can help you understand how light moves?**

- A thinking about how water moves
- B thinking about your favorite foods
- C thinking about your best friend
- D thinking about how animals move

_____ **2 What would happen if all light waves had the same amount of energy?**

- A They would not move.
- B They would not reflect.
- C We would not see different colors.
- D We would not see light at all.

_____ **3 Which object would probably reflect the *most* light?**

- A a brick
- B a smooth silver plate
- C a piece of ice
- D a slice of bread

_____ **4 What is this text *mostly* about?**

- A reflection
- B refraction
- C how we see
- D how light travels

_____ **5 Why can we see?**

- A Light can be absorbed.
- B Light waves bounce off objects and travel to our eyes.
- C Light cannot refract.
- D Light does not travel in waves.

_____ **6 When light waves bend, they are ___________**

- A reflecting.
- B being absorbed.
- C refracting.
- D brighter.

Word Power

Choose the English word from the Vocabulary list that correctly matches the definition.

the return of a wave of light

____

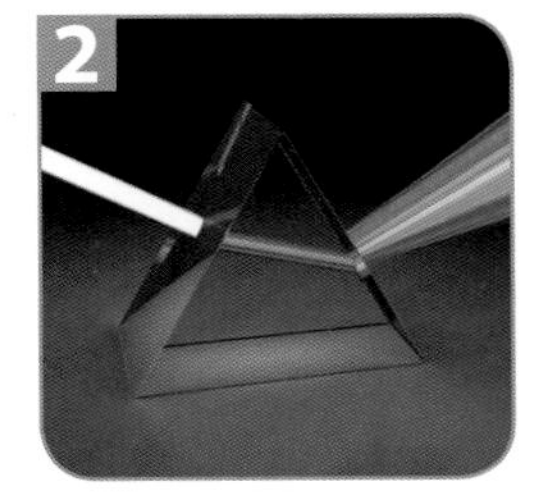

a bend in a light ray

____

to send out rays or waves

____

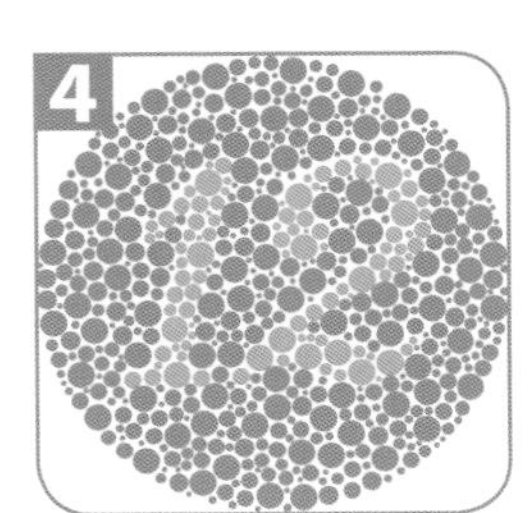

able to be seen

____

Reading Tip

Authors often choose language to convey a specific mood, to paint a particular image, or to clearly explain something. The language that an author uses often tells you a lot about what you are reading.

Skill Overview

Use of language refers to the devices and techniques that an author adds to a text to help readers acquire meaning. Examples include the use of **vivid verbs**, **strong adjectives**, **metaphor**, **point of view**, and **dialogue**.

RACE THE WIND

When the sand began kicking up and lashing our faces, I started to worry that maybe we should have left the beach. That afternoon, my dad had stood on the deck of our home and laughed as our neighbors **packed** up their cars and headed inland, out of range of the approaching summer storm. Challenging the weather to dampen our spirits, my sister, my mom, and I lit a fire on the beach while Dad told jokes and roasted marshmallows that tasted like bark.

Now, it was 6:30 p.m., and all laughter had evaporated. Our eyes were drawn to the sky, where a dark wall of clouds **marched** toward us. The red sunset bled through the storm clouds, turning the sky into a swirling **torrent** of dark fire. Below, the black waves of Lake Michigan **grappled** and slammed against each other as they sent icy tendrils toward the sky.

My sister, Kim, spotted it first. It was a **waterspout**—a tornado with a funnel made of water—and it was heading straight for us. The wind started screaming, and in a **flash** we were running toward the cottage. My mom stopped next to the front door of the tiny clapboard beach cottage. "Where can we go?" She shouted the question at my dad.

I turned to look at the sky. Now, instead of looking beautiful, it looked deadly. This liquid sister of the tornado wouldn't wait for us to get in the car and drive to safety.

"Under the deck!" my dad yelled. We **scrambled** beneath the deck, pressing ourselves against the foundation of the cottage, and then watched the approaching storm in silent terror. The 200-foot-high waterspout shot toward us, as if it had been fired from a cannon the size of the Sun.

My dad shouted "Hold on!" and something else I couldn't hear over the screaming wind.

The spout **sprinted** over the final stretch of water, an animal eager to make the kill. It lunged over the crashing waves, twisted through the blood-red sky, and then hit the beach. And then, like a monster of the night that is exposed to the Sun, the waterspout began to disintegrate when it hit land. By the time it reached our cottage, it was nothing more than a strong gust of water-colored wind that pelted our bodies. The rest of the storm raged for an hour and then simply blew away.

"Next time, we'll stay inland at Grandma's. Okay?" my dad said, tears of relief in his eyes. We all agreed that would be a good idea.

Vocabulary

pack
to put something into a bag, box, etc.

march
to walk somewhere quickly and in a determined way

torrent
heavy downpour of rain

✪**grapple**
to take hold of; to wrestle

✪**waterspout**
a tornado with a funnel made of water

flash
a brief time

scramble
to move or climb quickly but with difficulty

sprint
to run as fast as possible over a short distance

Reading Skill Comprehension Practice

Authors often use figurative language to describe ideas in a more vivid way. Here are three forms of figurative language.

Personification	Metaphor	Simile
This means giving human qualities to nonhuman things.	Authors often use it to compare two unlike objects.	A simile is a comparison that uses the word like or as.

Another way that authors use language to create a certain mood or image is through **dialogue**. A dialogue is a conversation between characters in a story.

Write examples of personification used in this passage.

Personification

01
sand began kicking up
and lashing our faces

02

03

04

Identify examples of a metaphor and a simile used in the passage.

Metaphor

Simile

Review the passage looking specifically at the dialogues and punctuation. Then answer the questions below.

1. How does the dialogue add to the passage?

2. What kind of emotions are behind the words?

3. Why do you think the author chose to use exclamation points within the dialogues?

Comprehension Review

Fill in the best answer for each question.

_____ **1** ***When the sand began kicking up and lashing our faces...***

This is an example of ____________.

- Ⓐ a simile.
- Ⓑ a metaphor.
- Ⓒ a poem.
- Ⓓ personification.

_____ **2** **Which is a metaphor used in this story?**

- Ⓐ The spout sprinted over the final stretch of water, an animal eager to make the kill.
- Ⓑ Dad told jokes and roasted marshmallows that tasted like bark.
- Ⓒ And then, like a monster of the night that is exposed to the Sun...
- Ⓓ We all agreed that would be a good idea.

_____ **3** ***And then, like a monster of the night that is exposed to the Sun...***

This ____________ compares the storm to a monster.

- Ⓐ metaphor
- Ⓑ personification
- Ⓒ alliteration
- Ⓓ simile

_____ **4** **What is the problem in this story?**

- Ⓐ The narrator is afraid of water.
- Ⓑ The family is caught in a tornado.
- Ⓒ The neighbors left.
- Ⓓ The family's car is gone.

_____ **5** **The family ____________ to stay safe.**

- Ⓐ gets in the car
- Ⓑ runs to the beach
- Ⓒ goes under the deck
- Ⓓ goes next door

_____ **6** **What is the purpose of this text?**

- Ⓐ to entertain readers
- Ⓑ to tell about something that happened
- Ⓒ to get readers to do something
- Ⓓ to give the narrator's opinion about something

Word Power

Choose the English word from the Vocabulary list that correctly matches the definition.

to take hold of; to wrestle

____

heavy downpour of rain

____

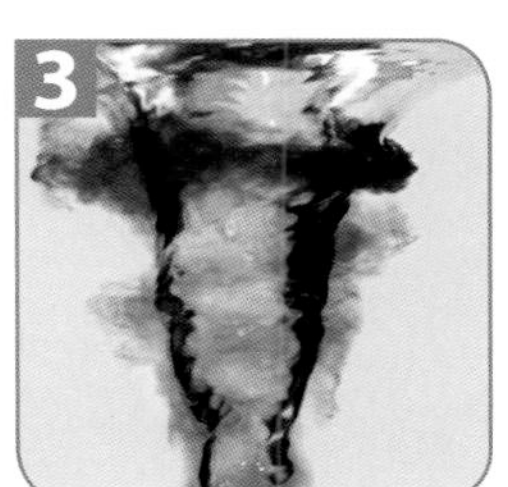

a tornado with a funnel made of water

____

to run as fast as possible over a short distance

____

FOR THE RECORD

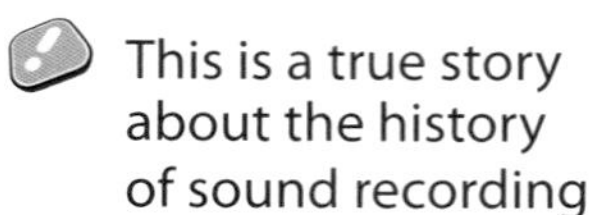

Reading Tip

- This is a true story about the history of sound recording machines.
- You can make use of a Venn diagram or a three-column chart to show information included in a compare-and-contrast text.

Skill Overview

Authors use a compare-and-contrast pattern to show similarities and differences. Readers may recognize this pattern by the use of certain signal words, such as **like**, **in comparison**, **opposite**, and **similar to**.

18

Thomas Edison made the first sound recording in 1877. He **recorded** himself singing "Mary Had a Little Lamb." At the time, people did not think Edison's **invention** would be useful. Many laughed at him. His recording machine seemed unbelievable. People thought that the only way to hear music was to be near a musician.

Edison's recording machine was called the *phonograph*. It was hard to use. To record sound and play it back, someone had to turn a crank exactly 60 times a minute. If not, the recording wouldn't sound right.

The early recordings did not look like the ones we see today. They were cylinders covered with tinfoil. The phonograph had a needle

Edison with the phonograph

1877
Recording Cylinder

1948
LP

that **scratched** the sound into the tinfoil. The recordings were not very clear. They could only be played back a few times before **wearing out**.

Ten years later, Emile Berliner designed a better recording machine. It used a flat **disc** made of plastic. These "records" lasted a lot longer than the tinfoil cylinders. For the first time, people could buy music and play it over and over on a player.

Still, Berliner's records only held about two minutes of music. In 1948, Columbia Records introduced the LP. *LP* stands for long-playing record. One LP held up to 30 minutes of music per side. Long symphonies could now be recorded. The LP, which changed music recording all over the world, came at a good time. In the 1950s, popular music and culture were growing quickly. Musicians wanted to make recordings, and people wanted to buy them. The LP allowed radio stations to play different kinds of music.

By 1962, people could also buy music on **magnetic tapes**. These tapes were put into plastic cases called *cassettes*. Cassettes were cheap and much more **portable** than LPs. In 1979, Sony invented a portable machine that played cassettes. This allowed people to listen to music anywhere.

Three years later, compact discs, called *CDs*, were introduced. They sounded better than any other type of recording. CDs could hold more than an hour of music. By the 1990s, CDs had mostly **replaced** LPs.

In 1998, a new invention came on the market: an MP3 player. This device stores, organizes, and plays digital audio files. An MP3 player offers high-quality sound and is more versatile than a CD.

In 1877, people laughed at Edison's first scratchy recording. But his invention was the beginning of important changes in the way people share sounds and music.

Vocabulary

record
to store sounds

invention
something that has never been made before

scratch
to cut or damage a surface slightly with something sharp or rough

wear out
to become damaged

disc
a small, round piece of plastic

magnetic tape
a thin plastic ribbon coated with magnetic material on which sound or other information is stored

portable
light and small enough to be easily carried or moved

replace
to take the place of

1962
Cassette tape

1982
CD

1998
MP3 or digital audio

Reading Skill Comprehension Practice

Part 1 Explain how the author uses a compare-and-contrast pattern in the passage.

Part 2 Please list the differences and similarities between an LP and CD in the Venn diagram below.

LP	BOTH	CD
• Invented in 1948	• Round in shape	• Better than LPs

Part 3 Complete the chart below using complete sentences to compare and contrast the two inventions you wrote about in Part 2.

What Is Being Compared?

Similarities	Differences

Comprehension Review

Fill in the best answer for each question.

_____ **1 LPs and cassettes _____**
- Ⓐ are unhandy.
- Ⓑ played more music than Berliner's machine could play.
- Ⓒ were invented in 1979.
- Ⓓ hold much more music than CDs.

_____ **2 Unlike CDs, cassettes _____**
- Ⓐ are made of magnetic tapes.
- Ⓑ sound better than any other kind of recording.
- Ⓒ hold more music than any other kind of recording.
- Ⓓ are more portable than LPs.

_____ **3 Edison's phonograph and Berliner's recording machine _____**
- Ⓐ used tinfoil cylinders.
- Ⓑ used flat discs.
- Ⓒ were portable.
- Ⓓ allowed people to listen to music without being near a musician.

_____ **4 What has happened to recordings since Edison's phonograph?**
- Ⓐ They have gotten much shorter.
- Ⓑ They are much harder to hear now.
- Ⓒ The sound has gotten much better.
- Ⓓ People have stopped listening to music.

_____ **5 Which statement is false?**
- Ⓐ LPs were introduced in 1948.
- Ⓑ The first sound recording was made by Sony Music.
- Ⓒ By the 1990s, CDs had mostly replaced LPs.
- Ⓓ Until 1877, the only way to hear music was to be near a musician.

_____ **6 The author wants readers to _____**
- Ⓐ know about changes in the way people share sounds and music.
- Ⓑ buy CDs.
- Ⓒ learn about Thomas Edison.
- Ⓓ know that CDs are not a good way to listen to music.

Word Power

Choose the English word from the Vocabulary list that correctly matches the definition.

1

a small, round piece of plastic

____

2

to take the place of

____

3

a thin plastic ribbon coated with magnetic material on which sound or other information is stored

____

4

light and small enough to be easily carried or moved

____

What Is a Biome?

Skill Overview

A reader's prior knowledge includes background information on the subject as well as his or her life experiences. When readers are able to make connections between what they already know and what they are reading, reading comprehension is enhanced.

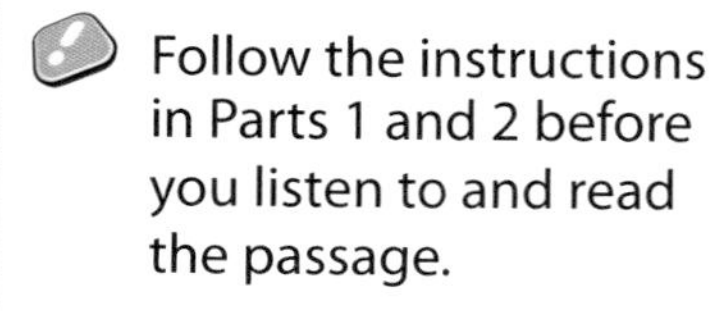

Follow the instructions in Parts 1 and 2 before you listen to and read the passage.

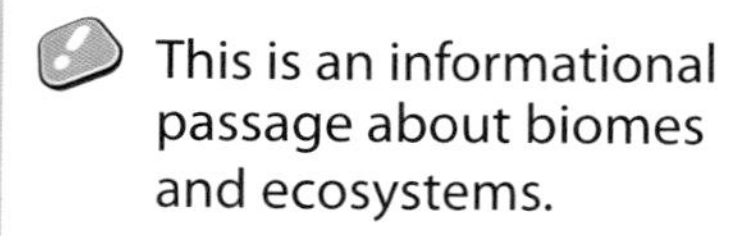

This is an informational passage about biomes and ecosystems.

19

Earth has different areas called *biomes*. Each **biome** has its own **climate**. For example, a desert has dry weather and sand or rocks instead of soil. This affects the kinds of plants and animals that can live there.

Altitude and **latitude** determine biome **boundaries**. Altitude measures how high a place is. Latitude helps determine how hot a place is.

Altitude measures the height above sea level. It affects what can grow. For example, trees will grow only up to the tree line on a mountain. Above that, it is too windy and cold. Most of the soil has blown away, leaving only rocks. Only short plants can grow in this alpine biome. Sheep, elk, chinchillas, and birds live here and eat these plants.

Latitude measures the **distance** from the equator. The equator is an invisible line around the middle of Earth. The closer a place is to the equator, the hotter the weather. The farther away from the equator, the cooler the weather gets.

In the far north, summers are too short and cool for trees. Only short grass, lichens, and mosses grow in the tundra biome. These plants can do photosynthesis at low temperatures with long spells of daylight. Caribou eat the grasses, and polar bears may eat the caribou.

Near the equator, the average temperature is around 25°C (77°F) year-round. It rains all the time. This is where you will find **tropical** rain forests. Tropical rain forests have millions of different plants and animals. They cover less than seven percent of the land on the planet, yet they **support** more than half the Earth's plant and animal species!

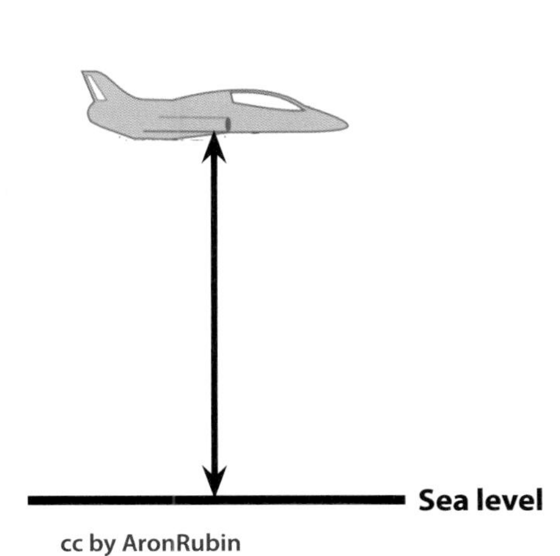

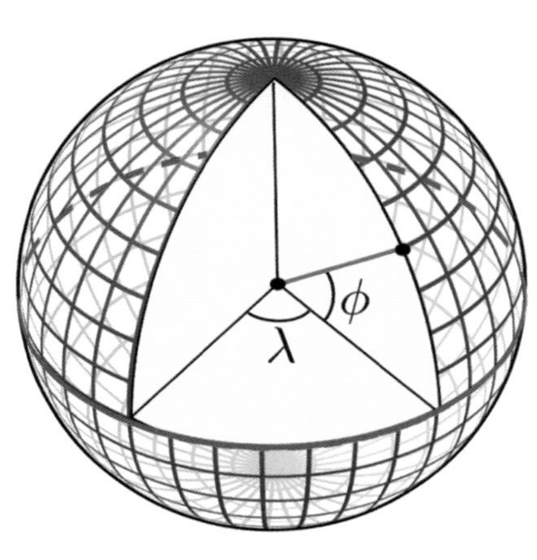

Figure showing the definitions of latitude (φ) and longitude (λ) on a sphere.

Vocabulary

- **✪biome** an area in nature with its own climate
- **climate** the general weather conditions typically found in a particular place
- **altitude** height above sea level
- **latitude** distance north or south of the equator
- **boundary** a real or imagined line that marks the edge or limit of something
- **distance** the amount of space between two places
- **tropical** extremely hot and humid
- **support** to provide the right conditions, such as enough food and water, for life

Reading Skill Comprehension Practice

Part 1 **Describe a time when you read or learned something that helped you adjust or extend your knowledge about the topic.**

Part 2 **Brainstorm what you already know or think about the topic of this passage. Record your ideas in the web.**

Biomes

1. *Biomes are found all around the world.*

2.

3.

4.

Part 3 **Now that you have read the entire passage, tell how your knowledge of this topic has changed.**

Comprehension Review

Fill in the best answer for each question.

_____ **1 Remembering what you know about __________ helps you learn more about that particular biomes.**

- Ⓐ a rock
- Ⓑ the desert
- Ⓒ a river
- Ⓓ a bird

_____ **2 You already know that it is cold high up in the mountains. You can use this information to better understand ______**

- Ⓐ why deserts are dry.
- Ⓑ tropical rain forests.
- Ⓒ how altitude affects climate.
- Ⓓ why the rain forests cover less than seven percent of Earth's surface.

_____ **3 If you remember that tropical rain forests are located near the equator, you will better understand ______**

- Ⓐ how latitude affects climate.
- Ⓑ how altitude affects climate.
- Ⓒ how animals affect climate.
- Ⓓ animals of the desert.

_____ **4 Which feature would you probably *not* see in an alpine biome?**

- Ⓐ sheep
- Ⓑ short plants
- Ⓒ a palm tree
- Ⓓ many rocks

_____ **5 Why is most of the United States *not* tropical?**

- Ⓐ It is too large.
- Ⓑ It is too far away from the equator.
- Ⓒ It is too close to the equator.
- Ⓓ It has an alpine climate.

_____ **6 Biomes are mostly affected by ______**

- Ⓐ animals and plants.
- Ⓑ length and width.
- Ⓒ altitude and latitude.
- Ⓓ oceans and deserts.

Word Power

Choose the English word from the Vocabulary list that correctly matches the definition.

1

height above sea level

____

2

a real or imagined line that marks the edge or limit of something

____

3

distance north or south of the equator

____

4
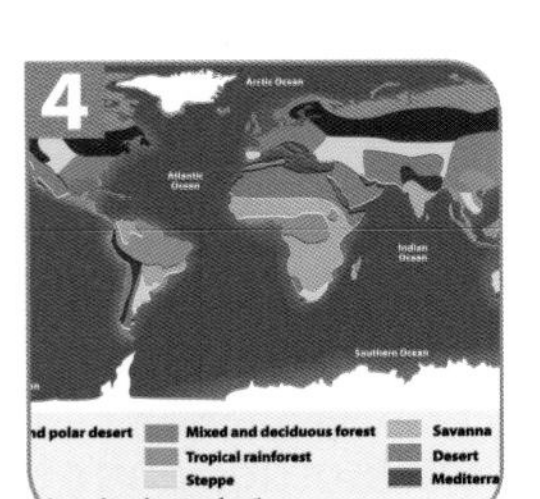

an area in nature with its own climate

____

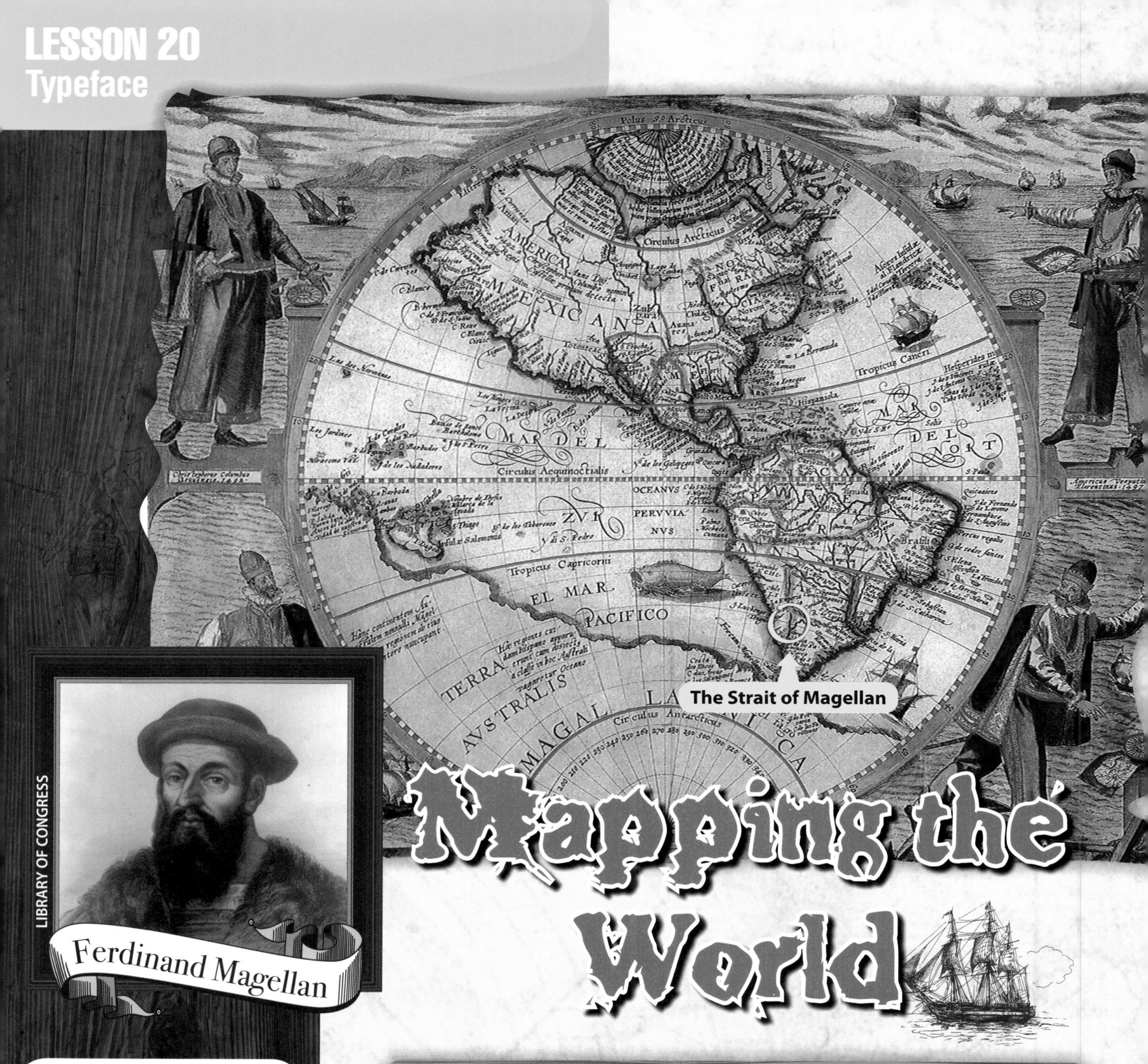

Mapping the World

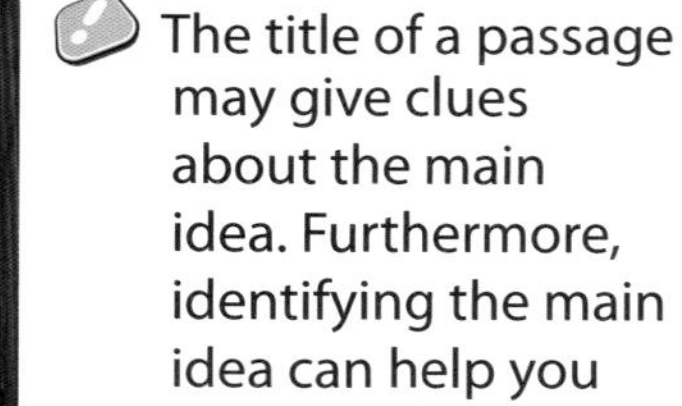

Reading Tip

The title of a passage may give clues about the main idea. Furthermore, identifying the main idea can help you better understand the passage.

Skill Overview

Typeface refers to the different kinds of text used to share information with the reader, including different **sizes**, **styles**, and **colors** of text. Successful readers use typeface to help determine main ideas and to locate information in a text.

20

Kings and queens always wanted to **conquer** new lands. Each **monarch** wanted to **spread** his or her empire. Explorers were sent to find new trade **routes** as they traveled across the world. Trading with other countries helped monarchs become powerful.

To help trade, it was important to have good maps. However, Europeans hadn't visited some parts of the planet. So no one really knew how large Earth was. Back then, maps of the world looked very different than they do today. Mapmakers tried to guess the size of Earth, but they were not always right.

The Trip Around the World

For a long time, European ships had to sail around the southern tip of Africa to get to the islands of Southeast Asia. Ferdinand Magellan was a Portuguese **navigator**. He thought he could find a shortcut to these islands. So he **sailed** west from Spain with five ships and 270 men. He thought that going across the Atlantic Ocean would be a shorter **distance** than going around Africa.

In South America, he discovered a narrow **strait** near the continent's southern tip. His maps showed Japan as only 200 miles (322 km) from Mexico. It was only then that Magellan told his crew that he had decided to sail around the world! The crew almost starved to death before landing in the Philippines on the other side of the Pacific Ocean.

Unfortunately, Magellan died in a war against a tribe in the Philippines. He never saw Spain again. Later, only one ship and 18 men made it back to Spain. They were the first people to sail around the world.

Vocabulary

conquer
to take control by force

monarch
a king or queen

spread
to cover, reach

route
a particular way or direction between places

navigator
one who steers a ship or directs its course

sail
to control a boat that has no engine and is pushed by the wind

distance
the amount of space between two places

strait
a narrow channel connecting two large bodies of water

A Long Journey

Did you know that it took the men three years to make this trip around the world? While crossing the ocean, the crew was so hungry that they ate rats found on the ship.

Magellan's crew discovering the Strait of Magellan

Reading Skill Comprehension Practice

Part 1 Think about how the typeface used in the passage helps a reader who may be looking at the page for the first time. Record your ideas below.

Part 2 Explain how different kinds of typeface can be useful to readers.

Part 3 Note the different typeface used in the title of this passage. This gives the reader a clue about the main idea of the text. What do you think the main idea of the text is? Write your ideas below.

Mapping the World

Comprehension Review

Fill in the best answer for each question.

_____ **1 Why is the title of the passage in the largest typeface?**
- A It gives a clue about the main idea.
- B It is not a sentence.
- C It is not important.
- D It gives someone's name

_____ **2 Based on the typeface used, which of these is an important idea?**
- A Trading with other countries helped monarchs become powerful.
- B The Trip Around the World
- C The crew almost starved to death before landing in the Philippines on the other side of the Pacific Ocean.
- D Later, only one ship and 18 men made it back to Spain.

_____ **3 The typefaces in the passage would help a person _____**
- A learn about Magellan.
- B learn why trade was important.
- C find out how many men Magellan had with him.
- D decide what this passage is about.

_____ **4 What happened to Ferdinand Magellan?**
- A He became the king of Spain.
- B He became England's greatest hero.
- C He was killed in the Philippines.
- D He made five trips around the world.

_____ **5 Which of these sentences is true?**
- A The trip around the world took two weeks.
- B Magellan's crew was the first to sail around the world.
- C A long time ago, maps looked exactly as they do now.
- D Nobody in Magellan's crew ever made it back to Spain.

_____ **6 Magellan and his crew ran out of _____ on their trip.**
- A clothes
- B rope
- C tools
- D food

Word Power

Choose the English word from the Vocabulary list that correctly matches the definition.

1

one who steers a ship or directs its course

_____

2

a narrow channel connecting two large bodies of water

_____

3

to control a boat that has no engine and is pushed by the wind

_____

4

to take control by force

_____

Three-Way Tie

Reading Tip

- Authors usually write texts with a particular purpose in mind.
- Think about what techniques the author uses to accomplish his or her purpose.
- One way an author accomplishes a purpose is through **word choice**, another way is through **style**.

Skill Overview

Authors' devices include giving specific examples, using dialogue, choosing specific points of view, using characterization, varying punctuation, and using figurative language. Authors use specific devices in order to accomplish their purposes.

He is home. Once his key unlocks the door, his role changes from businessman to father. Our father. Three steps behind the dog (who always hears the jingling keys first), we three boys run upstairs. We **soar** into his arms, clutch his legs, and hang like chimpanzees from his tie. This gives him an **incentive** to remove it and change into "Daddy" clothes, comfortable and comforting. He becomes a bridge, and we crawl over and under, fighting for kisses, rejecting the kisses, but wanting more. Meetings, deadlines, and decisions **vanish** faster than the setting Sun.

As the last of us is pried off, **clinging** tighter than a barnacle to the underside of a fishing trawler, we four "men" stumble into the kitchen. There, food not only nourishes, but also provides time to talk about the day. Dad always asks the questions, and we are **eager** to share our news and our world with him.

Our family adventures include places where picnics can be brought and distances where we drift into dreamland in the car, yet always wake up in our own beds. School events are attended by both Mom and Dad, hand in hand, and Dad never complains about missing work.

Somehow, he **manages** to coach our sports. A whistle, a navy sweat suit, and a baseball cap are his **trademarks**. Untied cleats are the only **indication** that his dressing isn't done in the team locker room, but at the office. His cell phone beeps in the glove compartment. At the end of practice or a game, one of us might see the blinking light and hand Dad the phone. Dad always responds, "You boys are my business." And he returns the phone to its spot.

The "roughhousing" of the past has become arm wrestling matches and running races. Dad now needs a partner on the basketball court instead of the three-on-one competitions. Whether our teams win the trophies or whether we make the team, we three boys know we are Dad's first-place prizes. He always tells us when he grabs the three of us in a bear hug, "My three-way tie." We squirm and resist, but hold him tighter as he whispers again, "My three-way tie."

Vocabulary

soar
to reach a great height

incentive
reward for doing something

vanish
to disappear or stop being present or existing

cling
to hold on tightly

eager
wanting very much to do or have something

manage
to succeed in doing something

trademark
a characteristic, feature, or way of dressing that identifies a particular person

indication
a sign that something is true

Reading Skill Comprehension Practice

Part 1 Explain the author's **purpose** for writing this passage.

The purpose of this author is . . .

power up

There are different purposes for writing, including to **inform**, **persuade**, and **entertain**.

Part 2 Reexamine the passage, and then explain how the author's **word choice** helps accomplish his purpose for writing this passage.

The author uses words to . . .

Part 3 Explain how the author's **style** helps accomplish his purpose for writing this passage.

The author's style of writing . . .

Comprehension Review

Fill in the best answer for each question.

_____ ❶ **What device does the author use to describe how the boys greet their father?**

Ⓐ persuasion
Ⓑ foreshadowing
Ⓒ similes and metaphors
Ⓓ personification

_____ ❷ **How does the author describe his father?**

Ⓐ as angry
Ⓑ as frightened
Ⓒ as sad
Ⓓ as loving

_____ ❸ **You can tell a great deal about the author's father because the author uses __________**

Ⓐ many examples.
Ⓑ irony.
Ⓒ sarcasm.
Ⓓ setting.

_____ ❹ **What does the father mean when he says, *"You boys are my business"*?**

Ⓐ He wants to know everything the boys are doing.
Ⓑ The boys are the most important thing in his life.
Ⓒ The boys are busy.
Ⓓ The boys help him with his work.

_____ ❺ **What is most important to the author's father?**

Ⓐ his job
Ⓑ sports
Ⓒ his family
Ⓓ money

_____ ❻ **What can you infer about the author and his brothers?**

Ⓐ They like sports.
Ⓑ They are angry at their father.
Ⓒ They do not like the outdoors.
Ⓓ They have never played baseball.

Word Power

Choose the English word from the Vocabulary list that correctly matches the definition.

reward for doing something

____

a sign that something is true

____

a characteristic, feature, or way of dressing that identifies a particular person

____

to hold on tightly

____

Reading Tip

Think about the point of view used by the author as you listen to and read this passage.

From Boredom to Bird Watching

Skill Overview

Point of view refers to **the perspective that a piece of literature expresses** to its audience. Usually the point of view is assigned to the narrator, and the story is told from a first-person or third-person perspective.

22

It was a class trip, and I had to go. Otherwise, you'd never catch me hiking through the woods, swatting mosquitoes and belting blackflies while **attempting** to "record nature" in my **journal**.

Three days in the **wilderness** (the correct term is *our environment*) without electricity! Portable radios weren't allowed. Shampoo was unnecessary. The bathhouse had only three toilets and a sink large enough for Smokey the Bear. The boys' and girls' camps were separated by the dining hall and miles of snake-infested **terrain**.

On the first day, we had **mandatory** activities: orienteering, fire building, plant identification, first aid, and shelter building. Camping in my backyard is the closest I'll ever get to camping again. No need to know how to **construct** a branch and twig shelter there. On the second day, we could pick our own activities—like Mountain Biking, Celebrate Thoreau, and Bog Jog. I chose Bird Watching. I figured it would include a nice hike and a nicer place to rest. Boy, was I wrong!

A five-mile hike left me with barely a squeeze of hydrocortisone cream. Ducking the underbrush had my hair follicles crying for soap. The climb burned my thighs, and my hamstrings ached. PE was easy compared with this. But when we reached the top, I forgot about my itching and hamburger craving. We were on a cliff of white quartz, streaked with silver. We actually looked down on the pine trees. The clouds were touchable, and I had never been so close to the Sun or seen the blue of a sky like that.

I thought a bird was a bird, but again I was wrong. We saw cedar waxwings and ovenbirds. We saw turkey vultures, bluebirds, warblers, and woodpeckers. I had seen chickadees and goldfinches at our bird feeder. But these birds, along with the sparrows and cardinals, never looked more beautiful.

My journal was full of sketches, information, and . . . poems. Me! I've never been inspired to write a poem, let alone share it with others! Our **descent** was too quick. We talked about the differences among birds—from the songs they sang to the way they looked. At the bathhouse, I heard an ovenbird, "Chirp, chirp, chirp!" I tried to find him, but before I knew it, the dinner horn was blaring angrily—I didn't even have time to shampoo!

But the following morning, the horn from the bus was much more disturbing. I hated to **admit** it, but I wasn't ready to go home!

Vocabulary

attempt
to try to do something

journal
a written record of what you have done each day

wilderness
an outside area in which plants are left to grow naturally or untidily

✪**terrain**
a specific type of land

mandatory
must be done

construct
to build something or put together different parts

descent
the way down

admit
to agree that something is true

Reading Skill Comprehension Practice

power up

First person

- **limited** point of view
- told by one character and always uses words such as *I*, *me*, *my*, *us*, and *we*

Third person

- **omniscient** point of view
- told by a narrator who is separate from the characters of the story and uses words such as *he*, *she*, and *they*

Part 1 Answer the questions below.

1. What is the **point of view** of the passage?

____

____

2. Which **words or phrases** indicate the point of view of the passage?

____

____

3. Why do you think the author chose this point of view?

____

____

4. Did it help make the story more interesting? Why or why not?

____

____

Part 2 Think about how the narrator presents a limited point of view. What possible information about the story is **not** given by this character? Write your ideas below.

____

____

____

Part 3 Write a short story about yourself using **first-person** point of view.

____

____

____

____

____

Comprehension Review

Fill in the best answer for each question.

____ **1 At the beginning of the story, the narrator ________**

Ⓐ loves to hike and camp.
Ⓑ does not like the wilderness.
Ⓒ believes that camping is exciting.
Ⓓ thinks that showering is not necessary.

____ **2 Which event changes the narrator's point of view?**

Ⓐ a bus ride
Ⓑ a swim in the lake
Ⓒ a forest fire
Ⓓ a bird-watching hike

____ **3 You can tell the narrator's point of view has changed when he ________**

Ⓐ says that the birds are beautiful.
Ⓑ complains about the five-mile hike.
Ⓒ goes to sleep.
Ⓓ decides that camping in the backyard is fun.

____ **4 *Our descent was too quick.* What does this sentence really mean?**

Ⓐ The hikers had to run.
Ⓑ The narrator was enjoying the hike and wanted to keep hiking.
Ⓒ The hills were too steep.
Ⓓ The narrator got sick from moving too fast.

____ **5 What did the narrator do for the first time on this hike?**

Ⓐ take a shower
Ⓑ run
Ⓒ write a poem
Ⓓ see birds

____ **6 The narrator chose bird watching because he ________**

Ⓐ loves birds.
Ⓑ wanted the exercise.
Ⓒ was used to long hikes and camping.
Ⓓ thought there would be time to rest.

Word Power

Choose the English word from the Vocabulary list that correctly matches the definition.

1

the way down

____

2

must be done

____

3

a specific type of land

____

4

an outside area in which plants are left to grow naturally or untidily

____

How the Sons Filled the Hut

(A Russian Tale)

Reading Tip

- Please follow the instruction in Part 1 before you listen to and read the passage.
- This story is a folktale It may have a lesson to offer you, which may not be entirely realistic.

Skill Overview

When a reader draws conclusions, he or she is determining additional information based on the facts presented in the text. Successful readers also rely on past experience and prior knowledge to help them draw conclusions.

In a small village, there was once a father who had three sons. Two were thought to be **clever** fellows, but the third was so **simple** that everyone said the lad was a fool.

One day, the father decided to build a **hut** at the edge of his pasture. When the small house was finished, he called his sons together and said, "I will give this hut to the one who can fill it completely. Not even a **corner** is to be left empty."

The oldest son said, "I know the very thing that will do it."

And off he went to buy a horse. When he brought the animal into the new hut, the horse filled only one corner of the place.

At once, the second son hurried off, saying, "I know the very thing that will fill this hut."

He returned with a load of **hay**, which he **hauled** into the new hut. The hay filled only half of the little house.

The youngest son scratched the top of his head with one hand. "I suppose it's my turn to try my luck," he said slowly, trudging off into the village. There he **wandered** about for the rest of the day.

Toward evening, as the lights began to shine from the cottage windows, the young lad suddenly slapped his thigh and laughed out loud. "Now I know the very thing that will do it!" he **exclaimed**.

Like a flash, he bought a fat candle and hurried to the new hut.

Once inside, the lad lit the candle—and lo!—the whole hut was filled with light—every corner, nook, and cranny. And so, the simple son, who everyone thought was a fool, won the new little house for himself.

Vocabulary

clever
quick in learning; inventive

simple
lacking in intelligence

hut
a small, plain building, usually consisting of one room

corner
the point or area that is formed by the meeting of two lines, surfaces

hay
grass that is cut and dried and used as animal food

haul
to pull or drag with effort

wander
to walk around without any clear purpose or direction

exclaim
to say or shout something suddenly, with surprise

Reading Skill Comprehension Practice

power up

Explicit
refers to information that is clearly stated in a text

Implicit
refers to information that is understood but not directly stated

Part 1 Record any conclusions you can draw about the passage based on its title *How the Sons Filled the Hut (A Russian Tale)*

1. I can conclude that some solutions will be provided in the passage.

2. ______

Part 2 Answer the questions below.

1. How would you describe the third son at the **beginning** of the story?

______

2. What do you think this story teaches you?

______

3. Why does the father challenge his sons in this unique way?

______

4. How would you describe the third son at the **end** of the story?

______

Part 3 Write two examples of explicit and implicit information in the passage.

Explicit Information	Implicit Information
______	______
______	______

Comprehension Review

Fill in the best answer for each question.

_____ **1 The villagers probably thought that ________**

Ⓐ the youngest son would win the hut.
Ⓑ the youngest son was very intelligent.
Ⓒ the youngest son would not win the hut.
Ⓓ the father liked the youngest son best.

_____ **2 The other sons were probably ________ when the youngest son won the hut.**

Ⓐ not surprised
Ⓑ very surprised
Ⓒ relieved
Ⓓ grateful

_____ **3 This story probably takes place ________**

Ⓐ in an apartment in a big city.
Ⓑ in a very large castle.
Ⓒ near an ocean.
Ⓓ on a farm near a tiny town.

_____ **4 What gave the youngest son his idea for filling the hut?**

Ⓐ lights in the cottage windows
Ⓑ the horse his brother put in the hut
Ⓒ his father's pasture
Ⓓ something he heard in the village

_____ **5 Which of these happened *first*?**

Ⓐ The youngest son won the hut.
Ⓑ The oldest son put a horse in the hut.
Ⓒ The father offered the son to the one who could fill it.
Ⓓ The second son brought hay to the hut.

_____ **6 What is the purpose of this passage?**

Ⓐ to tell a story
Ⓑ to get readers to visit a village
Ⓒ to tell something that happened to the author
Ⓓ to teach about Russian villages

Word Power

Choose the English word from the Vocabulary list that correctly matches the definition.

lacking in intelligence

____

to pull or drag with effort

____

quick in learning; inventive

____

to say or shout something suddenly, with surprise

____

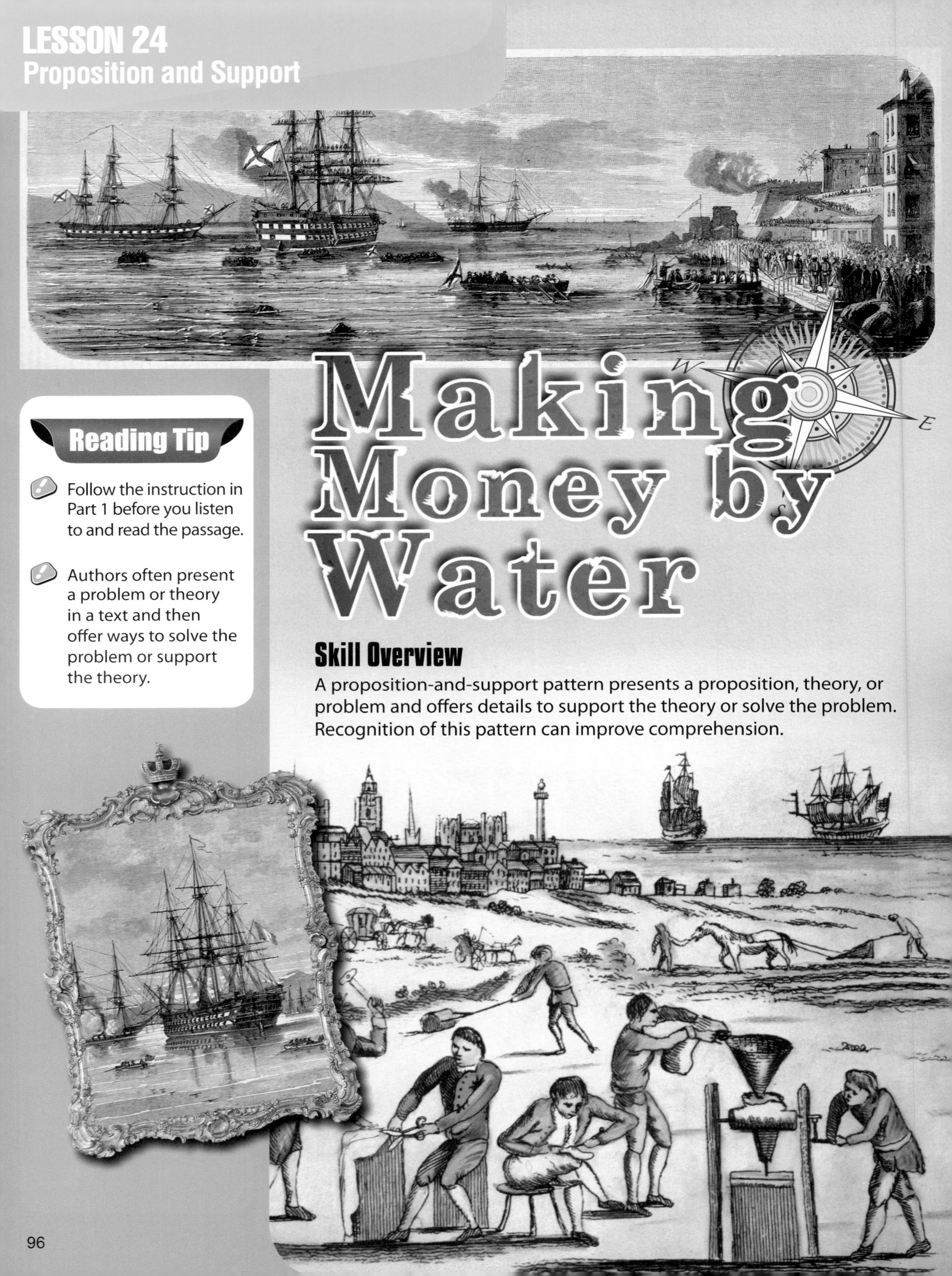

Making Money by Water

Reading Tip

- Follow the instruction in Part 1 before you listen to and read the passage.
- Authors often present a problem or theory in a text and then offer ways to solve the problem or support the theory.

Skill Overview

A proposition-and-support pattern presents a proposition, theory, or problem and offers details to support the theory or solve the problem. Recognition of this pattern can improve comprehension.

After arriving in the northern part of the New World, the **settlers** quickly learned that their new land was not very good for farming. The soil was rocky, and the winters were terribly long. They could grow only enough food to feed their own families. The settlers would have to be **resourceful** and find other ways to make a living. Because most of the settlers lived in towns along the ocean, it made sense that men would become shipbuilders, traders, and fishermen.

They made good use of the resources in the area to **survive** and prosper. The forests provided trees for building ships. The many animals living in the forests helped fur traders become rich.

Merchants traded with the British and with other **colonies**. They shipped furs, iron, lumber, fish, tobacco, and rice to Great Britain. In return, England shipped tools, guns, furniture, cloth, fine china, teas, and silks to the New World.

Fishermen in the **port towns** provided food for the region by catching clams, oysters, cod, and halibut. Some men also hunted whales. Whale blubber fueled oil lamps. The skin of the whales was made into purses and bags. The bones around the whales' mouths were used for combs and women's corsets.

Despite the **rough** conditions, the settlers found a way to **thrive** in their new home by the water.

Vocabulary

settler
a person who arrives in a new place, especially a new country, in order to live there and use the land

✪ **resourceful**
capable of finding a way to do something

survive
to continue to live or exist

merchant
a person whose job is to buy and sell products in large amounts

colony
a group of people living in a new land who are still ruled by a parent government

✪ **port town**
a town on the water, near where ships load or unload cargo, or goods

rough
uncomfortable; difficult

thrive
to grow, develop, or be successful

Reading Skill Comprehension Practice

Describe a possible problem or theory; then supply a solution for the problem or evidence to support the theory.

Problem / theory: ______________________________

Solution / support: ______________________________

Fill in the chart below with examples from the passage.

Proposition	Support
1. *Because most of the settlers lived in towns along the ocean, it made sense that men would become shipbuilders, traders, and fishermen.*	**1.** *Fishermen in the port towns provided food for the region by catching clams, oysters, cod, and halibut. Some men also hunted whales.*
2. ______________________________	**2.** ______________________________

Please answer the questions below using the passage RACE THE WIND in Lesson 17.

1. What is the **problem** in this text?

____

2. What is the **solution**?

____

3. Did the author include one solution or many solutions?

____

4. What is another solution for the problem?

____

Comprehension Review

Fill in the best answer for each question.

____ **1 According to the passage, what was the settlers' problem?**

- Ⓐ There were not enough of them to settle their new home.
- Ⓑ Their new land was not good for farming.
- Ⓒ They did not know how to farm.
- Ⓓ They could not find materials to build houses.

____ **2 *...It made sense that these men would become shipbuilders, traders, and fishermen.***

Which sentence supports this proposition?

- Ⓐ Some men also hunted whales.
- Ⓑ Merchants shipped many goods to Great Britain.
- Ⓒ Whale blubber fueled oil lamps.
- Ⓓ Most of the settlers lived in towns along the ocean.

____ **3 Which was a solution to the settlers' problem?**

- Ⓐ to farm the land
- Ⓑ to use whale bones for combs and women's corsets
- Ⓒ to find other ways to make a living
- Ⓓ to use whale blubber for oil lamps

____ **4 Where did shipbuilders get their wood?**

- Ⓐ from forests
- Ⓑ from the British
- Ⓒ from fur traders
- Ⓓ They did not use wood.

____ **5 Which items were *not* made from whales?**

- Ⓐ purses and bags
- Ⓑ combs and women's corsets
- Ⓒ oil lamps
- Ⓓ ships

____ **6 How did the climate affect the settlers' ability to make a living?**

- Ⓐ The climate made it difficult for fur trading.
- Ⓑ The climate was perfect for farming.
- Ⓒ The climate made it very difficult to farm.
- Ⓓ The climate was too harsh for the settlers, so they could not settle there.

Word Power

Choose the English word from the Vocabulary list that correctly matches the definition.

a group of people living in a new land who are still ruled by a parent government

____

a town on the water, near where ships load or unload cargo, or goods

____

capable of finding a way to do something

____

to continue to live or exist

____

Turning the Tide for Sea Turtles

Reading Tip

An author often includes certain features that help you better understand the text. **Picture captions** are one such feature.

Skill Overview

Captions help readers better understand what they are reading by clarifying the text or by providing additional information. Successful readers notice and use picture captions to determine a text's main idea.

As evening falls, the light grows dim on La Escobilla (es-koh-BEE-yuh) Beach in Mexico. Slowly, thousands of sea turtles **emerge** from the waves. They **crawl** across the sand on unsteady flippers. Each is returning to the beach where it was born many years before. The turtles are back to lay their eggs.

La Escobilla Beach is in Oaxaca (woh-HAH-kah), Mexico. It is a big nesting ground for olive ridley sea turtles. Every year, many olive ridleys come ashore to build their nests and lay their eggs. This happens from June to December. Then the turtles cover the eggs with sand and return to the ocean. In 45 days, the babies **hatch** and scamper into the ocean. "It's phenomenal," says biologist Wallace J. Nichols.

Baby olive ridley sea turtle

ADRIANA ZEHBRAUSKA / POLARIS

Thousands of olive ridley turtles arrive to lay their eggs on La Escobilla Beach in Mexico

This has occurred for about 150 million years. Turtles have outlived dinosaurs, but they're no match for modern predators. Many turtles are killed by poachers, or illegal hunters. Poachers kill them for their meat and shells, and they also take their eggs. Some turtles get caught in fishing nets. Others are killed by pollution.

Turtle Protection

Today, the world's **population** of sea turtles has become very small. Scientists are worried about two of the **species** that live in the Pacific Ocean. These two species are the loggerhead and the leatherback turtles. They fear that these species will be extinct in 30 years if nothing is done.

But a program in Mexico shows that turtles can survive. At La Escobilla and Morro Ayuta (eye-YOU-tuh), the olive ridley population is going up. These are two major nesting beaches for the turtles. Officials expect that there will be about one million olive ridley nests at La Escobilla. That's four times as many as there were in 1990 when sea turtle hunting was banned in Mexico.

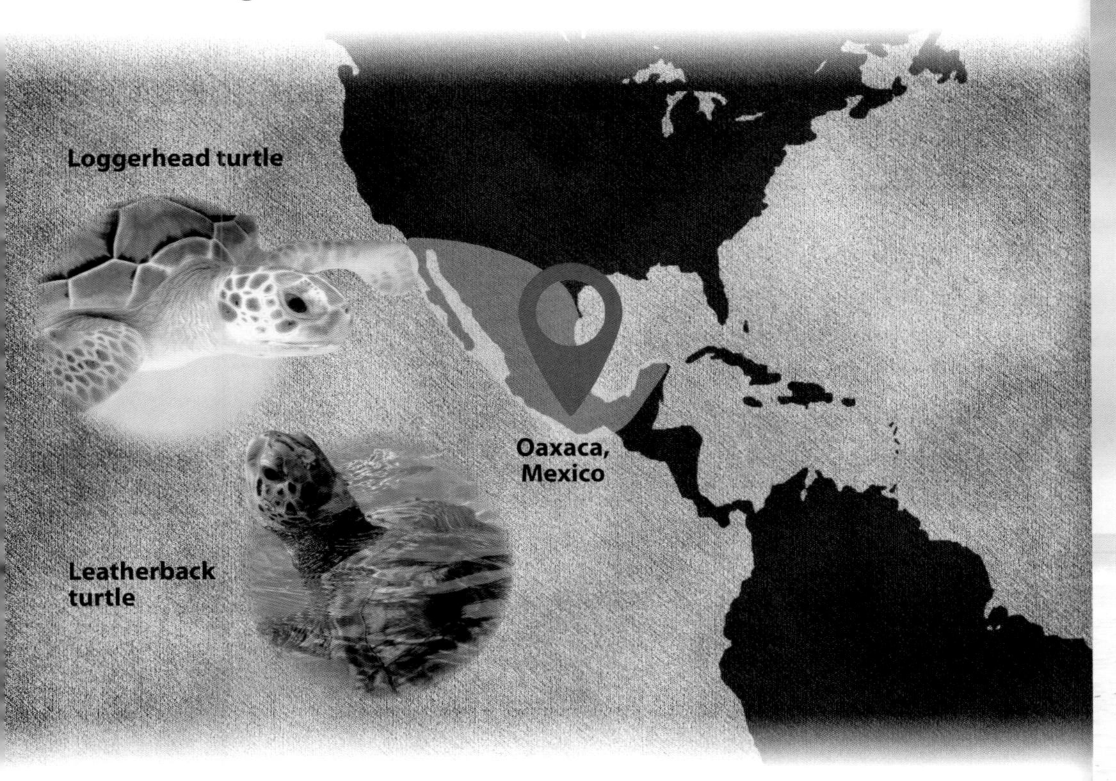

The exciting change came about through community education and tough tactics. At the Turtle Center near La Escobilla, kids and adults learn about turtle **protection**. In addition to the hunting **ban**, officials **patrol** area beaches. They guard nesting turtles and their eggs.

Today, poachers still sell turtle products. But the community is trying to help the animals. People are learning that a healthy and large turtle population attracts tourists. Tourists bring money to the area. As one community member says, "When the people understand that they can benefit from the turtles, they want to help the turtles."

Vocabulary

emerge
to appear by coming out of something or out from behind something

crawl
to move slowly or with difficulty

hatch
to break out of an egg

population
the number of organisms in a group (such as a type of animal or a group of people)

species
a group of animals with similar characteristics

protection
the act of keeping someone or something safe

ban
to forbid

patrol
to go around an area or a building to see if there is any trouble or danger

Reading Skill Comprehension Practice

Leatherback turtle

A **picture caption** describes what is happening in the picture or who is pictured. The caption can include facts or clues to help readers make inferences about the text.

Explain how the pictures and captions help you better understand this passage.

Suppose the author wanted to describe more about the olive ridley sea turtles using the picture captions. What might the captions say? Write an example on the lines below.

Answer the questions below based on Lesson 20, Mapping the World.

1. Copy one of the picture captions from the passage.

2. How does the picture caption help you understand the text?

3. Why is it important to include picture captions?

Comprehension Review

Fill in the best answer for each question.

_____ **1 The pictures and captions tell you that this is passage *mainly* about**

____

- Ⓐ sea turtles.
- Ⓑ La Escobilla beach.
- Ⓒ Mexico.
- Ⓓ sea turtle hunting.

_____ **2 Which information is learned from a picture caption in the passage?**

- Ⓐ La Escobilla beach is a great tourist attraction.
- Ⓑ The sea turtles are dying.
- Ⓒ Thousands of sea turtles lay eggs at La Escobilla beach.
- Ⓓ The sea turtles return to Mexico in July to lay eggs.

_____ **3 Which sentence from the passage *best* relates to the picture caption on the bottom right of page 100?**

- Ⓐ At La Escobilla, the olive ridley population is going up.
- Ⓑ Every year, many olive ridleys come ashore to build their nests and lay their eggs.
- Ⓒ But the community is trying to help the animals.
- Ⓓ Today, poachers still sell turtle products.

_____ **4 Which of these is not used to protect turtles in Mexico?**

- Ⓐ community education
- Ⓑ a hunting ban
- Ⓒ a rescue center for sea turtles
- Ⓓ beach patrols to guard nesting turtles

_____ **5 *They fear that these species will be extinct in 30 years.***

What does <u>*extinct*</u> mean as used in this sentence?

- Ⓐ will no longer exist
- Ⓑ will no longer be killed for their meat and shells
- Ⓒ will no longer be a tourist attraction
- Ⓓ will no longer lay their eggs on the beach

_____ **6 About how long does it take for a sea turtle baby to hatch?**

- Ⓐ 30 days
- Ⓑ 45 days
- Ⓒ 30 years
- Ⓓ 60 days

Word Power

Choose the English word from the Vocabulary list that correctly matches the definition.

the number of organisms in a group (such as a type of animal or a group of people)

____

the act of keeping someone or something safe

____

a group of animals with similar characteristics

____

to break out of an egg

____

Ancient Egypt

Reading Tip

- Please follow the instruction in Part 1 before you listen to and read the passage.
- Different strategies can be used to help clear up confusing parts of a text, such as **pausing**, **rereading**, **drawing on background knowledge**, and **asking for help**.

Skill Overview

Successful readers know when information in a text is confusing. It is important for readers to be aware and monitor their reading so that when there is confusion, it can be clarified. Clarifying confusing parts of a text will lead to better comprehension of the information.

canopic jars

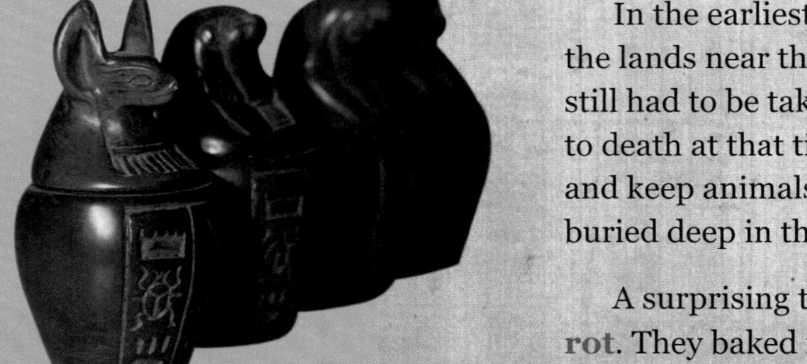

26

In the earliest days of Egypt, **tribes** of nomads wandered the lands near the Nile River. The bodies of those who died still had to be taken care of. There was no **ceremony** attached to death at that time. However, to **remove** bodies from sight and keep animals away, the remains of people who died were buried deep in the hot desert sand.

A surprising thing happened. The buried bodies did not **rot**. They baked in the extreme heat of the sand so that they dried out. The people still looked much like they had in life.

{heart} Rhody's photos via Getty Images

Vocabulary

tribe
a group of people, often of related families, who live together, sharing the same language, culture, and history

ceremony
a set of formal acts, often fixed and traditional

remove
to take out

rot
to decay

discovery
the act of finding out something that was unknown

corpse
a dead body

remain
to stay in the same place

treat
to deal with something in a particular way

This **discovery** led to *mummification*. How could you dry out a body but keep it where animals or floods would not uncover it? The answer was *natron*, a natural salt that dries out a **corpse** and leaves it quite lifelike.

Creating a Mummy

There were several steps in creating a mummy. First, embalmers removed the vital organs. Only the heart **remained** in the body. It would be needed when the mummy returned to life. The other internal organs were placed in a clay canopic jar.

The body was then **treated** with natron and wrapped in hundreds of yards of linen. About 20 layers of wrapping were needed. Often, the dead person's jewelry was placed between the layers of wrapping.

The body was then placed in a decorated casket. It was hidden in a burial chamber along with the treasures of the deceased.

Reading Skill Comprehension Practice

Think about times when you have used strategies to correct mistakes while reading. Write your thoughts about these strategies below.

I have drawn on background knowledge to correct mistakes while reading. For example . . .

Answer the questions below.

1. What strategies did you use with this passage?

With this passage, I used . . .

2. How did using the strategies help you understand the passage?

Think about other strategies you used (or have used in the past) that have helped you to clarify confusion while reading. Write about your experiences below.

Comprehension Review

Fill in the best answer for each question.

____ **1 If you did not know what the word *corpse* means, how could you find out?**

- Ⓐ Spell the word.
- Ⓑ Skip the word and read on.
- Ⓒ Write the word a few times.
- Ⓓ Reread the sentence to figure it out.

____ **2 What should you do to learn how to pronounce words such as canopic?**

- Ⓐ Read the rest of the text.
- Ⓑ Write the word.
- Ⓒ Look up the word in a dictionary.
- Ⓓ Read the sentence again.

____ **3 If you forgot what *natron* is, what could you do?**

- Ⓐ Read the third paragraph again.
- Ⓑ Read more of the text.
- Ⓒ Write the word.
- Ⓓ Read the word out loud.

____ **4 The author wants readers to ____**

- Ⓐ learn an Egyptian recipe.
- Ⓑ travel to Egypt.
- Ⓒ learn about ancient Egyptian beliefs.
- Ⓓ save the environment.

____ **5 How did the ancient Egyptians discover mummification?**

- Ⓐ They looked in the Nile River.
- Ⓑ They found out that bodies buried in the hot desert sand dried out.
- Ⓒ They wandered through the desert.
- Ⓓ They used caskets.

____ **6 Which was the *first* step in making a mummy?**

- Ⓐ The body was covered in natron.
- Ⓑ The priests wrapped the body in linen.
- Ⓒ The dead person's jewels were placed between the layers of linen.
- Ⓓ Embalmers removed the vital organs.

Word Power

Choose the English word from the Vocabulary list that correctly matches the definition.

1 the act of finding out something that was unknown

____

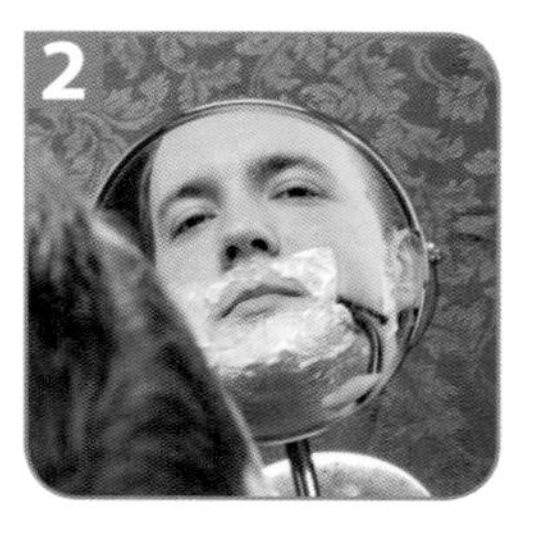

2 to take out

____

3 a dead body

____

4 to decay

____

Skill Overview

Chapter titles can provide readers with valuable information and help them to understand and interpret text. Readers can use chapter titles to **determine the main idea**, **locate information**, or **make predictions**.

Reading Tip

- This passage could have been taken from a book about North American tribes. The title can help you make predictions about the chapter.
- Follow the instruction in Part 1 before you listen to and read the passage.

Chapter 3: Early North American Tribes The Iroquois

An Iroquois longhouse

THE GRANGER COLLECTION

27

Life in a Longhouse

The Iroquois people lived in villages of **longhouses**. These were large wood-frame buildings covered with sheets of elm bark. Iroquois longhouses were up to 100 ft (30.5 m) long. Each one housed an entire clan (as many as 60 people). Each had two doors and no windows, with one door located at each end. Inside the longhouses, platforms were made for sleeping and for storage. The doors of each longhouse were carved or painted with the **symbol** of the clan or tribe who lived there. This was important because everyone in the clan was considered to be **related**—to be family.

FOOD

The Iroquois were farmers, fishermen, gatherers, and hunters. But most of their food came from farming. Iroquois women and children did most of the **farming** and **gathering**. They planted crops of corn, beans, and squash. They also harvested wild berries and herbs. The herbs were often used for medicinal purposes. The food was stored during the winter and usually lasted for two to three years. Iroquois men did most of the hunting—shooting deer, elk, and wild turkey. Fishing was also a major source of food because they lived near a large river. Iroquois dishes included cornbread, soups, and stews cooked on stone hearths.

THE GRANGER COLLECTION

Iroquois Country

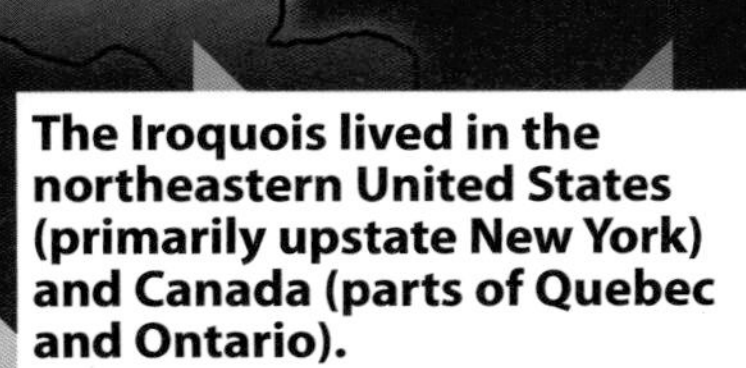

The Iroquois lived in the northeastern United States (primarily upstate New York) and Canada (parts of Quebec and Ontario).

WAMPUM

Because the Iroquois had no writing system, they relied on the spoken word to pass down their history, rituals, and traditions. In order to help them remember things, the Iroquois **crafted** wampum—white and purple beads made from the shell of a crab. Wampum were often arranged on belts in designs that represented significant events. They were also **traded** as a kind of **currency**, but they were more important culturally as an art material.

Vocabulary

✪longhouse
a long dwelling made by some North American Indian tribes

symbol
a sign, shape, or object that is used to represent something else

related
connected

farming
the activity of working on a farm or organizing the work there

gathering
the collecting of berries, leaves, fruits, etc., for food or other uses

craft
to make objects, especially in a skilled way

trade
to do business with

currency
an item used for bartering, such as paper money, shells, or gold

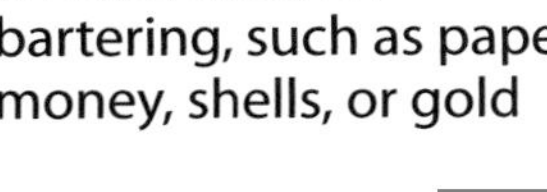

Reading Skill Comprehension Practice

Part 1 Use the chapter title below to make a prediction about the text that goes along with it.

EARLY NORTH AMERICAN TRIBES

I think this chapter will be about ______________________________

____

Part 2 The title **EARLY NORTH AMERICAN TRIBES** helps the reader know what the chapter is about. Write three other chapter titles that would send the same message to the reader.

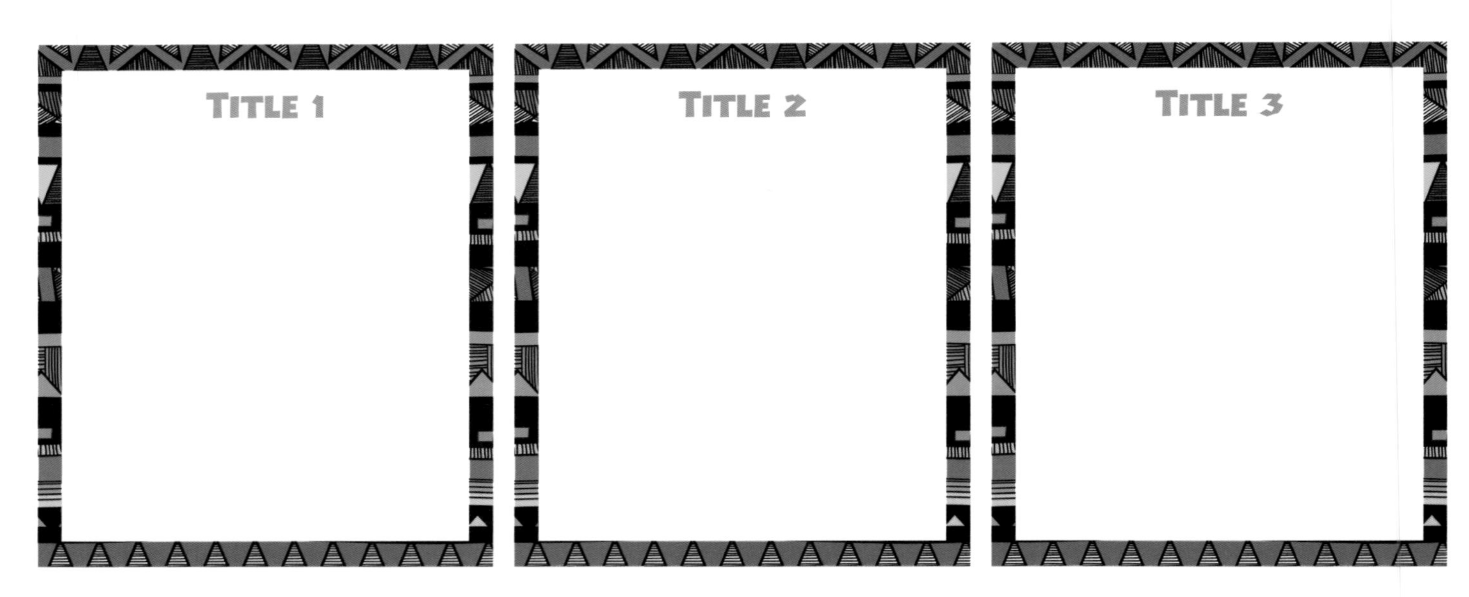

Part 3 Write the main idea of this passage.

____

____

____

Comprehension Review

Fill in the best answer for each question.

______ **1 The title tells you that this passage is *mostly* about ___________**

- Ⓐ how the Iroquois harvested food.
- Ⓑ an early North American Indian tribe.
- Ⓒ modern day American Indian tribes.
- Ⓓ how the Iroquois used wampum.

______ **2 In this passage, you learn about ___________**

- Ⓐ the culture and customs of early North American Indians.
- Ⓑ South American Indian tribes.
- Ⓒ the French and Indian War.
- Ⓓ how to make jewelry out of wampum.

______ **3 *The Iroquois***
This heading provides another meaning clue. It tells you that you will read about ___________

- Ⓐ when the very first tribes settled in America.
- Ⓑ early North American tribes.
- Ⓒ how the Iroquois lived.
- Ⓓ how to tell the difference between Indian tribes.

______ **4 *Most* of the food that the Iroquois ate came from ___________**

- Ⓐ hunting.
- Ⓑ fishing.
- Ⓒ gathering.
- Ⓓ farming.

______ **5 The author wants you to ___________**

- Ⓐ learn about the customs of the Iroquois people.
- Ⓑ learn how to build a longhouse.
- Ⓒ visit the Iroquois people.
- Ⓓ learn how to farm and hunt.

______ **6 What is the *main* reason the Iroquois used wampum in their culture?**

- Ⓐ They used wampum as currency.
- Ⓑ They used wampum to represent significant events, as they had no writing system.
- Ⓒ They used wampum to trade with other tribes.
- Ⓓ They made jewelry out of wampum.

Word Power

Choose the English word from the Vocabulary list that correctly matches the definition.

1

an item used for bartering, such as paper money, shells, or gold

____

2

the collecting of berries, leaves, fruits, etc., for food or other uses

____

3

a long dwelling made by some North American Indian tribes

____

4

to make objects, especially in a skilled way

____

Reading Tip

Chronological order means that information is presented in the order in which the events occurred.

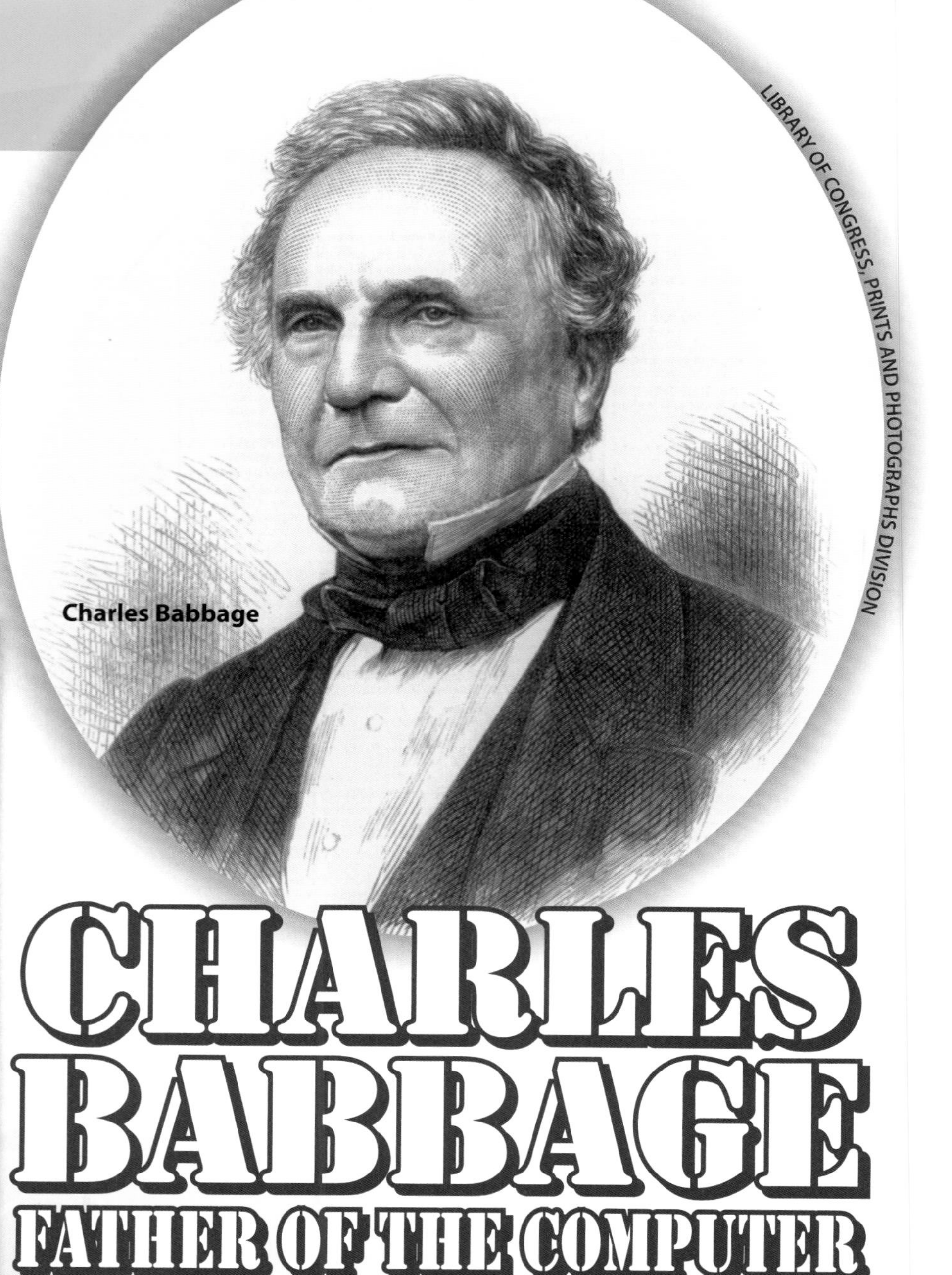

Charles Babbage

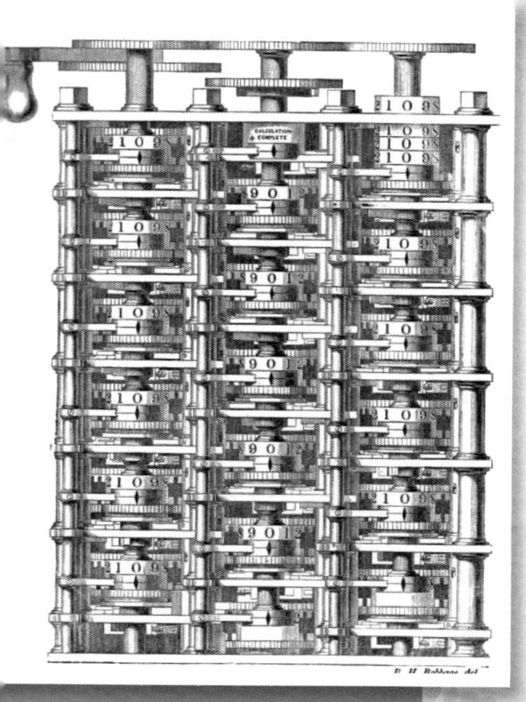

Difference Engine

CHARLES BABBAGE
FATHER OF THE COMPUTER

Skill Overview

Authors structure their writing so that readers can easily understand the information. **Chronological order** is often used for **historical or biographical texts**. An awareness of chronological order can help readers better understand a text.

Charles Babbage was born too soon. He hoped to **invent** a **mechanical** calculator. But the **technology** of his time was too simple. Babbage could not make his dream come true.

Babbage was born in London, England, in 1791. As a young boy, he liked doing math. He taught himself algebra, too. In college, he knew more about math than his teachers. After college, he taught math. He also founded the Royal Astronomical Society in 1820.

All his life, Babbage was **fascinated** by numbers. He asked people to mail him statistics. He wanted to know how fast a pig's heart beats. He wanted to make a table to **calculate** how much wood a man could saw in 10 hours. He thought that everything could be described in numbers.

Babbage was also an inventor. Around 1830, he decided to design and build a machine for doing mathematical calculations. He called this machine the *Difference Engine*.

MAKING THE MACHINE

Babbage's machine was **complicated**. It was made of two tons of brass, steel, and pewter gears. The wheels would crank out mathematical tables. While building it, Babbage decided he wanted the machine to be bigger. He wanted it to calculate figures to 20 decimal places.

Babbage kept working on the Difference Engine. Then he came up with an idea for a new machine. This one would do any mathematical task and any kind of calculation. He called the machine the *Analytical Engine*. It was the start of the modern computer. But Babbage did not complete either machine. He couldn't afford to continue his work.

THE LITTLE ENGINE THAT COULD

In 1854, two Swedish inventors built a working mechanical calculator. It was based on the Difference Engine. Their machine was able to print out different kinds of tables. It was very **accurate**.

Babbage went on working as a mathematician at Cambridge University. He also asked the government to donate more money toward math and science projects. Babbage was a **pioneer** in calculation. And he is more famous today than he was in his day.

Vocabulary

invent
to design or create something that has never been made before

mechanical
having to do with machines

technology
use of science to solve problems or make new machines

fascinated
very interested

calculate
to judge the number or amount of something

complicated
difficult to explain or understand

accurate
correct, exact, and without any mistakes

pioneer
one of the first people to do something

Reading Skill Comprehension Practice

Part 1 Explain why you think the author chose to write this passage in chronological order.

1. I think the author used chronological order to help readers understand this passage, which is a biography.

2. ______________________________

Part 2 List any clues within the text that tell the reader that this passage is written in chronological order.

There are dates in the passage.

Clues About Chronological Order

Part 3 List two other topics or texts that work well when written in chronological order.

1. biographies

2. ______________________________

3. ______________________________

Comprehension Review

Fill in the best answer for each question.

_____ **1 Which of these happened *last*?**

- **A** Babbage went to Cambridge University.
- **B** Babbage designed the Difference Engine.
- **C** Swedish inventors built a working calculator.
- **D** Babbage founded the Royal Astronomical Society.

_____ **2 Babbage designed his Difference Engine *after* ____________**

- **A** he couldn't afford to complete his work.
- **B** he designed the Analytical Engine.
- **C** two Swedish inventors built a Difference Engine.
- **D** he founded the Royal Astronomical Society.

_____ **3 Babbage's Analytical Engine was ____________**

- **A** designed after his Difference Engine.
- **B** built by two Swedish inventors.
- **C** created before his Difference Engine.
- **D** finally completed in 1879.

_____ **4 Which statement is true?**

- **A** Charles Babbage was a Swedish inventor.
- **B** The Analytical Engine was completed, but the Difference Engine was not.
- **C** Babbage worked at Cambridge University.
- **D** Babbage was not very interested in math or numbers.

_____ **5 Why did Babbage never complete his machines?**

- **A** Two Swedish inventors completed them first.
- **B** He could not afford to continue his work.
- **C** He was too busy with the Royal Astronomical Society.
- **D** He did not want to complete his machines.

_____ **6 Babbage's Difference Engine was ____________**

- **A** very easy to make.
- **B** originally designed by Swedish inventors.
- **C** his last project.
- **D** made of two tons of brass, steel, and pewter gears.

Word Power

Choose the English word from the Vocabulary list that correctly matches the definition.

1 difficult to explain or understand

____

2 very interested

____

3 having to do with machines

____

4 a person who is one of the first people to do something

____

Reading Tip

Follow the instruction in Part 1 before you listen to and read the passage.

Running Lobster Traps

Skill Overview

Facts are **true statements**; **opinions** reflect one's **feelings or emotions**. Fiction and nonfiction texts may include both facts and opinions. Successful readers distinguish between the two in order to read critically and understand an author's point of view.

Marcus enjoyed helping his uncle run his lobster **traps**. It was fun riding out in the flatboat, pulling up the heavy box traps and seeing if there was a lobster inside. His uncle **baited** each trap with a **morsel** of food that the lobster liked. When a lobster came along, it would smell the food and then push its way through the door at the end of the trap to get to it. Once it went in, there was no way out.

"How much do you know about our friend the lobster?" his uncle asked Marcus one chilly morning. They were **skimming** across the glassy water on their way home from the traps. Having made a large catch, his uncle was in a happy mood.

Vocabulary

trap
a device or hole for catching animals

bait
to put food on a hook or in a trap to catch something

✪**morsel**
a small piece of food

skim
to glide along the surface

tasty
having a strong and very pleasant flavour

surface
the outer or top part or layer of something

survive
to continue to live or exist

sink
to go down below the surface

"Not much, Uncle, except they are very **tasty** to eat," Marcus yelled back over the roar of the engine. His uncle chuckled. "A mother lobster lays thousands of eggs, which are attached under the curve of her tail for protection. She carries them there for up to a year. Finally, she shakes them free, and they float on the water's **surface**. Most are eaten by birds and other sea animals. The ones that **survive** finally get heavy enough to **sink** to the bottom. There, they hatch as baby lobsters, about one-third of an inch (0.8 cm) long. When they become adults, they can grow to 2 ft (0.6 m). That is when we catch them in our traps."

"Someday, I hope I am as good at catching lobsters as you are, Uncle," laughed Marcus.

Reading Skill Comprehension Practice

Write two facts and two opinions from the passage. Then think of a fact and an opinion that could have been included in the passage and write them down.

Facts	Opinions
1. Most baby lobsters are eaten by birds and other sea animals.	1. It was fun riding out in the flatboat.
2.	2.
3.	3.

Possible Fact	Possible Opinion

Write two facts and two opinions from the passage in Lesson 27.

THE IROQUOIS TRIBE

Facts	Opinions
1. The Iroquois were one of the early North American tribes.	1. Iroquois women must have been very strong and tough.
2.	2.
3.	3.

Comprehension Review

Fill in the best answer for each question.

_____ **1 Which one is Marcus's opinion?**

- Ⓐ "There, they hatch as baby lobsters."
- Ⓑ It was fun riding out in the flatboat, pulling up the heavy box traps and seeing if there was a lobster inside.
- Ⓒ "Finally, she shakes them free."
- Ⓓ When a lobster came along, it would smell the food and then push its way through the door.

_____ **2 Which of these can be proven?**

- Ⓐ "They are very tasty to eat. "
- Ⓑ It was fun riding out in the flatboat.
- Ⓒ "A mother lobster lays thousands of eggs, which are attached under the curve of her tail for protection."
- Ⓓ "How much do you know about our friend the lobster?"

_____ **3 Which sentence tells you what Marcus thinks?**

- Ⓐ "Not much, Uncle, except they are very tasty to eat," Marcus yelled back over the roar of the engine.
- Ⓑ "The ones that survive get heavy enough to sink to the bottom."
- Ⓒ His uncle baited each trap with a morsel of food.
- Ⓓ When they become adults, they can grow to a length of two feet.

_____ **4 Which one comes *first*?**

- Ⓐ "The ones that survive finally get heavy enough to sink to the bottom."
- Ⓑ "A mother lobster lays thousands of eggs, which are attached under the curve of her tail for protection."
- Ⓒ "That is when we catch them in our traps."
- Ⓓ "Most are eaten by birds and other sea animals."

_____ **5 People who are interested in __________ would probably like this passage.**

- Ⓐ cooking
- Ⓑ the history of fishing
- Ⓒ basketball and baseball
- Ⓓ catching lobsters

_____ **6 What is this story *mostly* about?**

- Ⓐ how lobsters grow and are caught
- Ⓑ Marcus's favorite hobbies
- Ⓒ Marcus's uncle
- Ⓓ how to cook lobster

Word Power

Choose the English word from the Vocabulary list that correctly matches the definition.

1 

to glide along the surface

____

2 

to put food on a hook or in a trap to catch something

____

3 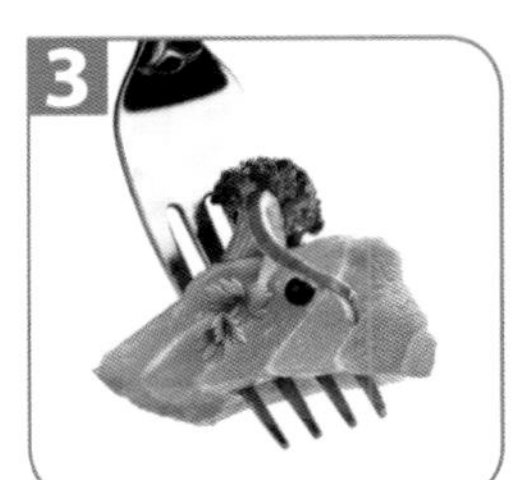

a small piece of food

____

4 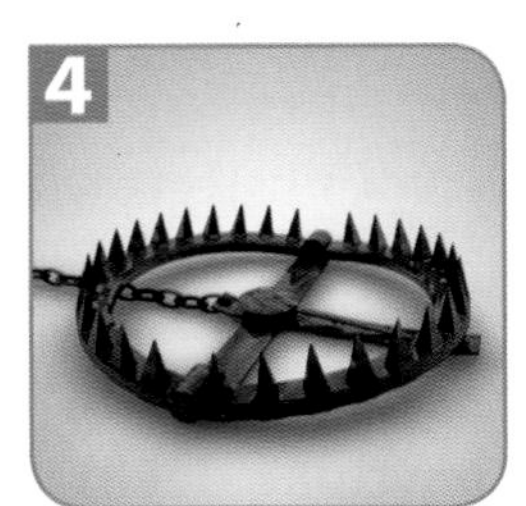

a device or hole for catching animals

____

Relativity

Skill Overview

Successful readers ask questions before, during, and after they read a text. When readers are actively engaged in a text and are thinking about questions as they read, they are monitoring their own comprehension and reading with a purpose.

Reading Tip

- Follow the instruction in Part 1 before you listen to and read the passage.
- Pause after each section to follow the instruction in Part 2.
- Asking questions helps you stay focused on the topic of the text and keeps you motivated to read further because you may have questions you want answered.

No Ether!

In 1905, Albert Einstein **published** a paper that explained his special theory of relativity. It solved a problem about how people understood light.

At the time, scientists believed that light waves worked like waves in the ocean. Ocean waves travel through the water. They thought light waves had to travel through something, too. They called this **substance** *ether*. There was one problem. Two scientists did an **experiment** to **measure** the ether. They couldn't find any.

Einstein's paper started with the work of other scientists. He used their math to explain that light did not need to travel through anything. Light was different from ocean waves. Light always travels

at the same speed. That speed is a very big number. Instead of always writing the number, Einstein just wrote *c*.

Space-time

Einstein wasn't done yet: Light was very different from ocean waves!

Imagine you are on a sailing ship, traveling alongside the waves. From your **perspective** on deck, the waves might appear to stop moving. You could even travel faster than the waves; then, the waves would appear to go backward!

Light works differently. Light always travels at *c*. Imagine you have a fast bicycle and your friend has a flashlight. Your friend shines the flashlight, and you pedal in the same direction. No matter how fast you go, the light will always shine ahead as if you were standing still.

Einstein said that the faster you go, the slower time goes and the shorter everything gets. The front of your bike will shrink back toward the end of your bike. The more you try to catch the light, the slower time goes and the shorter you get. We don't notice this in everyday life; it only happens close to the speed of light.

Einstein **demonstrated** that the old definitions of space and time needed to be changed. Because they are connected, Einstein **suggested** calling them *space-time*.

Vocabulary

publish
to have something you wrote printed in a book, newspaper, etc.

substance
material with particular physical characteristics

experiment
a test to find out what will happen

measure
to discover the exact size or amount of something

imagine
to form a mental picture or idea of something

perspective
your own way of looking at something

demonstrate
to show or make something clear

suggest
to mention an idea, possible plan, or action

Reading Skill Comprehension Practice

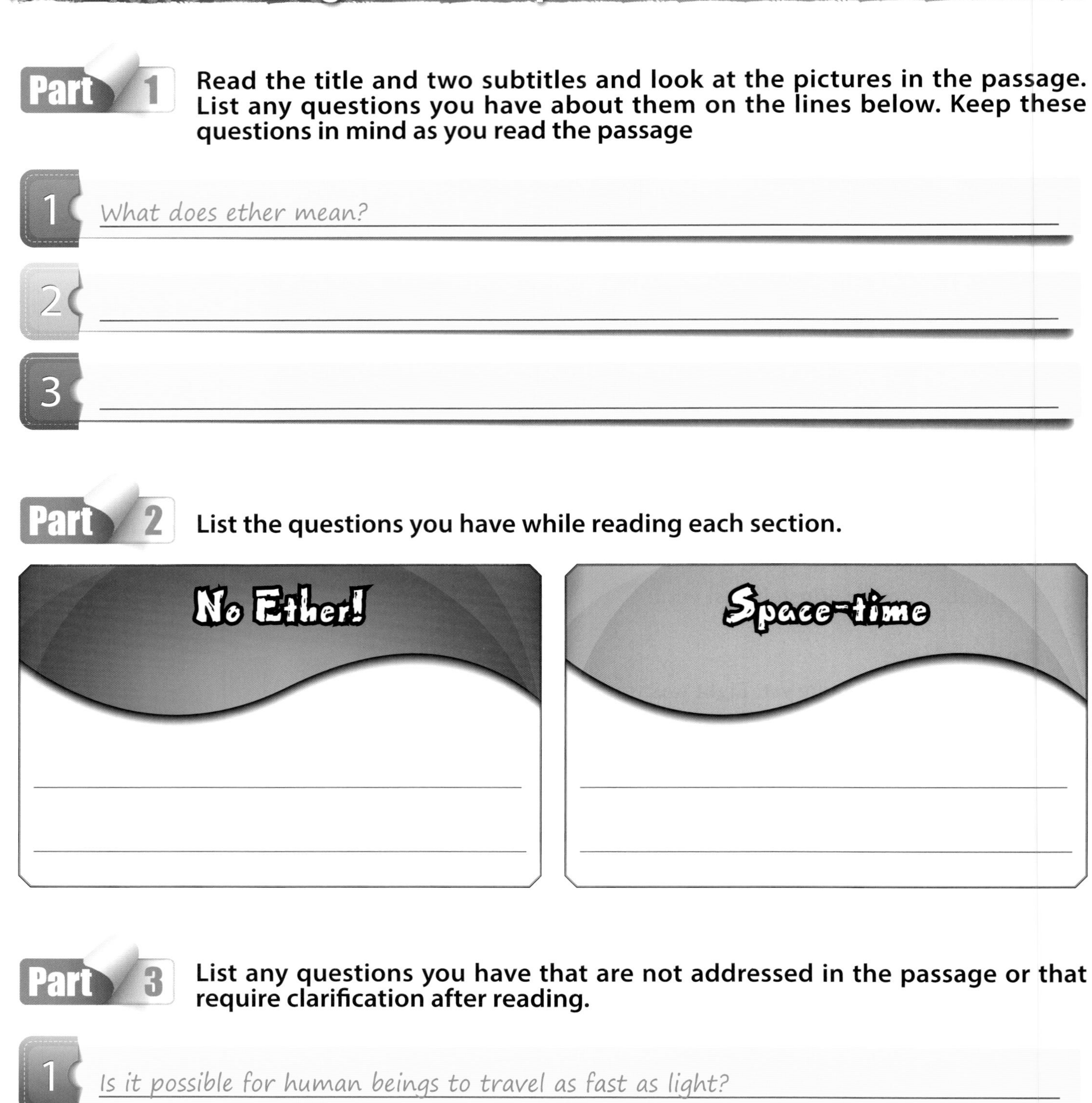

Part 1 Read the title and two subtitles and look at the pictures in the passage. List any questions you have about them on the lines below. Keep these questions in mind as you read the passage

1 *What does ether mean?*

2

3

Part 2 List the questions you have while reading each section.

No Ether!	Space-time

Part 3 List any questions you have that are not addressed in the passage or that require clarification after reading.

1 *Is it possible for human beings to travel as fast as light?*

2

3

Comprehension Review

Fill in the best answer for each question.

_____ **1 According to the first heading. What question can you predict the first section will answer?**

- Ⓐ What did Einstein do?
- Ⓑ What does *space-time* mean?
- Ⓒ What is ether?
- Ⓓ Where does light come from?

_____ **2 Which question is *not* answered in this passage?**

- Ⓐ How do light waves work?
- Ⓑ What number represents the speed of light?
- Ⓒ Are space and time connected?
- Ⓓ When did Einstein publish his paper on relativity?

_____ **3 *What did Einstein say about speed and time?***

Which sentence answers this question?

- Ⓐ Scientists used to think that light moved through ether.
- Ⓑ Einstein wasn't done yet: light was very different from ocean waves!
- Ⓒ Light works differently.
- Ⓓ Einstein said that the faster you go, the slower time goes.

_____ **4 Einstein's theory of __________ solved a problem about how people understood light.**

- Ⓐ relativity
- Ⓑ ether
- Ⓒ c
- Ⓓ space

_____ **5 Why don't we notice time slowing down and things getting shorter?**

- Ⓐ Ether prevents this from happening.
- Ⓑ Light waves do not work like ocean waves.
- Ⓒ This only happens close to the speed of light.
- Ⓓ Light waves work the same way as ocean waves.

_____ **6 Einstein believed that _____**

- Ⓐ light moves through ether.
- Ⓑ space and time are connected.
- Ⓒ light travels very slowly.
- Ⓓ light waves work the same way as ocean waves.

Word Power

Choose the English word from the Vocabulary list that correctly matches the definition.

1

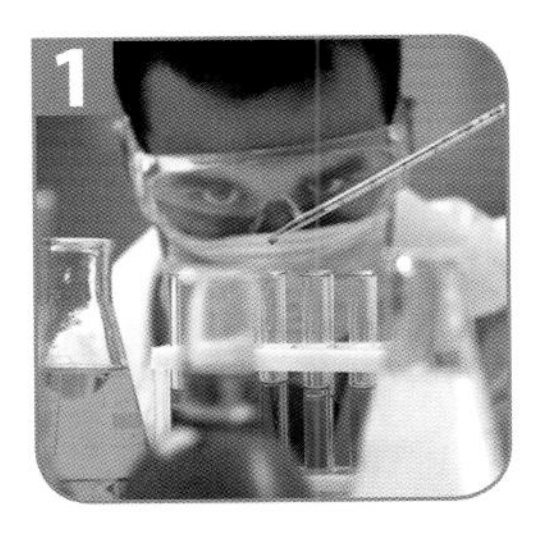

a test to find out what will happen

____

2

your own way of looking at something

____

3

to discover the exact size or amount of something

____

4

to have something you wrote printed in a book, newspaper, etc.

____

Review Test

Questions 1–9: Read the passage. Then turn the page and answer the questions. Fill in the letter next to the answer choice you think is correct.

Chapter 3: First Aid Safety

The Heimlich Maneuver

If you're not careful, you can choke on food that you're swallowing. When a piece of food blocks your windpipe, it can prevent you from breathing. When this happens, oxygen can't reach the brain. If the brain goes without oxygen for more than four to six minutes, it can die. So it is important to quickly expel any object that is causing a person to choke.

One way to do this is called the Heimlich (HYM-lick) maneuver. People have saved many lives by performing the Heimlich maneuver. That's why posters describing it hang on the walls of restaurants. Learn how to perform the Heimlich maneuver. You could use it one day to save a life.

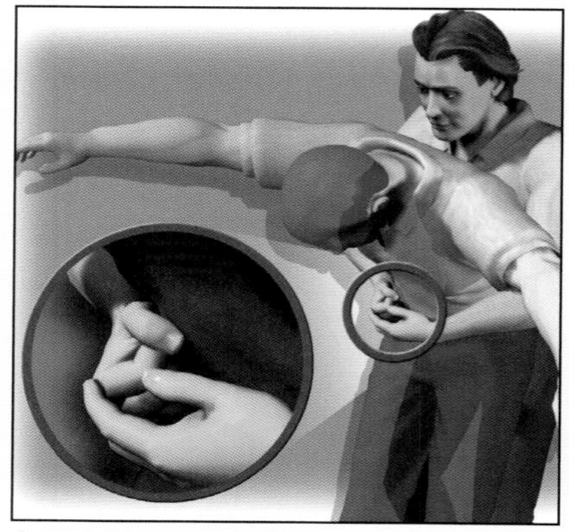

On another person.

On yourself

Illustrations by Rick Nease

1. If the choking person is conscious, quickly stand behind him or her. Put both arms around the person's waist. Make sure the person is bent forward a little.
2. Place one hand between the victim's naval, or belly button, and the rib cage. Make a fist, with the thumb facing the abdomen, or stomach area.
3. Place your other hand over your fist.
4. Using all your weight, press your open hand into your fist in a sharp upward movement. Your fist should push hard against the victim's abdomen.
5. If the object isn't ejected from the windpipe, repeat the procedure.
6. To perform the Heimlich maneuver on yourself, put your own fist above your navel. Place your other hand over your fist. Lean over a chair or countertop and use it as a lever to drive your fist into your abdomen. Make sure your fist is moving upward.
7. After the object is expelled, keep the victim still. Call for medical help. Even if the victim seems fine, he or she should be examined by a doctor.

1 *"Chapter 3: First Aid Safety"*
This chapter title tells you that you will read about ________ Lesson 27

- (A) things you can do when someone needs first aid help right away.
- (B) airplane safety.
- (C) skateboard safety.
- (D) the history of hospitals.

2 A preview of the pictures and titles tells you that this article is about ________ Lesson 2

- (A) how to cook a meal.
- (B) where to buy a chair.
- (C) how to help a choking person.
- (D) how air circulates in the lungs.

3 Which sentence tells the main idea of this passage? Lesson 5

- (A) The Heimlich maneuver can help a choking person, so it is a good idea to learn it.
- (B) The Heimlich maneuver is a very old method of saving choking people.
- (C) Start the Heimlich maneuver by putting your arms around the choking person's waist.
- (D) There are seven steps to the Heimlich maneuver.

4 The title is a good clue that this is about ________ Lesson 6

- (A) what makes a person choke.
- (B) how oxygen goes to the brain.
- (C) how the lungs work.
- (D) performing the Heimlich maneuver.

5 This would be a good choice to read if you wanted to ________ Lesson 7

- (A) find out how the body uses food.
- (B) learn how to help someone who is choking.
- (C) learn how oxygen travels in the body.
- (D) decide where to go for dinner.

6 In the Heimlich maneuver, place your other hand over your fist **after** ________ Lesson 9

- (A) performing the Heimlich maneuver on yourself.
- (B) repeating the procedure.
- (C) making a fist, with the thumb facing the abdomen.
- (D) pressing your open hand into your fist.

7 The heading for the image on the left tells you that this section is about ________ Lesson 10

- (A) helping someone else who is choking.
- (B) helping yourself if you are choking.
- (C) the history of the Heimlich maneuver.
- (D) how the lungs work.

8 *"One way to do this is called the Heimlich maneuver."*
This topic sentence is a clue that you will learn ________ Lesson 11

- (A) how the lungs and brain work.
- (B) what makes people choke.
- (C) where most people eat dinner.
- (D) the steps to performing the Heimlich maneuver.

9 Which sentence paraphrases Instruction #5? Lesson 14

- (A) Place your arms around the choking person's waist.
- (B) If the object isn't ejected from the windpipe, repeat the procedure.
- (C) If the object doesn't pop out, try the Heimlich maneuver again.
- (D) The Heimlich maneuver is one way to help a choking person.

Questions 10–19: Read the passage. Then answer the questions. Fill in the letter next to the answer choice you think is correct.

Hercules

Hercules is a great hero in Greek mythology. He was the son of Zeus, king of the gods of Olympia.

When Hercules was just a baby, he began showing that he had great strength. He killed two serpents that were about to attack him. As he grew up, he became famous for his strength and his kindness to those in need. He learned wrestling, archery, and fencing.

Although Hercules was basically a good person, he had one serious problem. He had a terrible temper. His temper was so uncontrollable that he was banished from Thebes. Hercules was told that the only way he could make up for his behavior was to serve King Eurystheus for 12 years. During this time, Hercules was given many difficult tasks to accomplish. With great determination, he was able to accomplish all of them.

10 How did Hercules resolve his conflict with the people of Thebes? Lesson 3

(A) He learned archery and swimming.
(B) He served King Eurystheus for 12 years.
(C) He was the son of Zeus, king of the gods of Olympia.
(D) He had a terrible temper.

11 The reason Hercules was so strong was probably that ________ Lesson 4

(A) he was kind to those in need.
(B) he became famous for his strength.
(C) he had a terrible temper.
(D) he was the son of Zeus.

12 Which one of these words **best** describes Hercules? Lesson 8

(A) athletic
(B) shy
(C) clumsy
(D) lazy

13 What piece of advice might you give to Hercules? Lesson 16

(A) Build up your strength.
(B) Be patient and don't get angry so quickly.
(C) If you see someone who needs help, offer help.
(D) Don't be so afraid of others.

14 What was the effect of Hercules' temper? Lesson 13

(A) He was made king.
(B) He was famous for his strength.
(C) He was banned from Thebes.
(D) He was kind to those in need.

15 One difference between Hercules and other people was that ________

Lesson 18

- (A) Hercules was much stronger than other people.
- (B) Hercules was the only man.
- (C) Hercules was basically a good person and other people were not good.
- (D) Hercules got angry and other people never did.

16 Which statement is probably true?

Lesson 22

- (A) This story is told from Hercules' point of view.
- (B) This story is told from King Eurystheus's point of view.
- (C) Hercules' point of view is that strength is not important.
- (D) From the people's point of view, Hercules' strength made him a hero.

17 You can conclude that ________

Lesson 23

- (A) King Eurystheus did not think Hercules was strong.
- (B) Hercules wanted to return to Thebes.
- (C) it wasn't easy to make Hercules angry.
- (D) Hercules never helped other people.

18 Hercules was banned from Thebes after ________

Lesson 28

- (A) his temper became uncontrollable.
- (B) he served King Eurystheus for 12 years.
- (C) he was given many difficult tasks to accomplish.
- (D) he was forced to leave Thebes.

19 Which question is **not** answered by this story?

Lesson 30

- (A) Why was Hercules banned from Thebes?
- (B) Whom did Hercules serve for 12 years?
- (C) What tasks did Hercules have to accomplish?
- (D) Why was Hercules famous?

Questions 20–30: Read the passage. Then turn the page and answer the questions. Fill in the letter next to the answer choice you think is correct

The Daily Trumpet

Editorial Page

Saving Our National Parks

Tourist traffic backs up at one of the entrances to Grand Canyon National Park

There is no more beautiful place in the world than Yellowstone National Park. Except maybe Denali National Park in Alaska. Or Grand Canyon National Park. Or the Fire Island National Seashore. The U.S. national park system is a true treasure that must be preserved. The United States is covered, from sea to shining sea, with cities and highways and factories. The amount of green areas is shrinking all the time. Private parkland is constantly being sold to developers. National parks are among the few places where nature is protected. They are oases where we can relax and commune with the wild. This untouched land allows people to understand what the area looked like hundreds of years ago, when it was pure and unspoiled. But the U.S. park system is in grave danger. The danger comes from two sources.

Tourist Time

Part of the problem is the many people who camp out in the parks. This glut of tourists is choking the parks with cars that cause pollution and run over animals. Poorly tended campfires have turned into wildfires, burning thousands of precious acres. Around coastal parks, powerboats harm and frighten wildlife, sometimes preventing them from mating. Oil spilling from the boats pollutes water. During the winter, the peace of the parks is broken by loud snowmobiles. In addition to noise pollution, they also bring air pollution, which kills plants and spoils the snow. At the entrance to Yellowstone Park, rangers need air pumped into their booths because the pollution is so bad!

What Can Be Done

The solution to this problem is clear. We think the park service must get tough with tourists. Drastically reduce the number of cars in the parks. Cut the number of snowmobiles allowed in parks. Forbid powerboats near coastal parks. Sure, some people will be outraged. But in the long run, they will be happy with the results.

But there is another problem that is much more dangerous than tourists are. To sum it up in a nutshell, the park system is being sold out to the private sector. Some parkland is being used for development. Soon, there may be private housing built on these once-untouchable preserves.

Another catastrophe is the opening of public land for oil drilling. The United States is far too reliant on foreign oil. And recent events make this reliance even more risky. But we must not let the need for one resource—oil—allow people to destroy another resource—these parks. We think the U.S. government should keep the parks from being overused and run down. They should also make sure the public lands will not be sold to private investors. Once the parks are gone, they won't return.

20 *"The U.S. national park system is a true treasure that must be preserved."*
This summary tells you that this passage is mainly about _______

Lesson 15

- (A) how and why people should preserve the U.S. national parks.
- (B) where to buy camping gear for a trip to a national park.
- (C) government officials.
- (D) where Yellowstone National Park is located.

21 *"The U.S. national park system is a true treasure that must be preserved. "*
The author uses this _______ to show how important the parks are.

Lesson 12

- (A) personification
- (B) onomatopoeia
- (C) simile
- (D) metaphor

22 What new information does this passage add to what you know about U.S. national parks?

Lesson 19

- (A) Animals live there.
- (B) They are in danger from too many tourists.
- (C) You can visit national parks.
- (D) National parks have many different kinds of trees.

23 The typeface tells you that _______ are a major problem for U.S. national parks.

Lesson 20

- (A) wild animals
- (B) park rangers
- (C) tourists
- (D) forests

24 Which tool does the author use to get you to agree that U.S. national parks should be preserved?

Lesson 21

- (A) persuasion
- (B) metaphor
- (C) symbolism
- (D) figurative language

25 Which detail supports the idea that pollution is dangerous to U.S. national parks? Lesson 24

- (A) Some parkland is being used for development.
- (B) The amount of green areas is shrinking all the time.
- (C) Oil spilling from the boats pollutes water.
- (D) National parks are among the few places where nature is protected.

26 *"Tourist traffic backs up at one of the entrances to Grand Canyon National Park."*
This caption is a clue that this passage is **mainly** about ________ Lesson 25

- (A) the climate in the U.S. national parks.
- (B) the best time to visit the U.S. national parks.
- (C) the history of the Grand Canyon.
- (D) the effect of tourists on U.S. national parks.

27 *"But the U.S. park system is in grave danger."*
If you didn't know what causes the danger to the U.S. parks, you could ________ Lesson 26

- (A) look for a list of national parks.
- (B) read more of the passage to find the information.
- (C) look on a map to find Yellowstone National Park.
- (D) reread the title of the passage.

28 You would probably read this passage to ________ Lesson 1

- (A) learn about the animals in the national parks.
- (B) find out about volunteering at a national park.
- (C) learn where the national parks are located.
- (D) learn someone's point of view about saving the national parks.

29 *"To sum it up in a nutshell"* means ________ Lesson 17

- (A) to eat nuts.
- (B) to put something in a nutshell
- (C) to get to the main point.
- (D) to write a summary sentence.

30 Which of these sentences is a fact? Lesson 29

- (A) But the U.S. park system is in grave danger.
- (B) Some parkland is being used for development.
- (C) There is no more beautiful place in the world than Yellowstone National Park.
- (D) We think the park service must get tough with tourists.

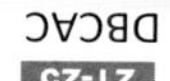

Answers

1-5	6-10	11-15	16-20	21-25	26-30
ACADB	CADCB	DABCA	DBACA	DBCAC	DBDCB